THE FAKE DATE

"You're making him up," Danny DePuzo said. "There isn't anybody."

"Oh, yes, there is."

"Janet does not tell lies," Karen said. Which is true, too.

They were all looking at me, and I could see Danny trying to find a loophole somewhere so he could stick my head in it.

"It's your uncle," he said.

I shook my head. "No relative."

Danny lifted his right hand. "You *swear* you asked a boy to go with you to the dance at Roosevelt, and you swear he said yes?"

I lifted my hand too. "I swear."

"Well, all I can say then is, that the world is full of weirdos," Danny said.

Karen sniffed. "You should know, Danny DePuzo."

I felt great as I looked at all their faces. I'd fooled them. Now, how was I going to get out of it?

Bantam Books for Young Readers that you'll enjoy
Ask your bookseller for the books you have missed

A WHOLE SUMMER OF WEIRD SUSAN by Louise Ladd
BOARDWALK WITH HOTEL by Claudia Mills
DAPHNE'S BOOK by Mary Downing Hahn
THE GHOST IN THE THIRD ROW by Bruce Coville
LOVE LETTERS TO MY FANS by Jackie Parker
NUTTY FOR PRESIDENT by Dean Hughes
TAFFY SINCLAIR AND THE ROMANCE MACHINE
   DISASTER by Betsy Haynes
THE GREAT MOM SWAP by Betsy Haynes
TIME FLIES! by Florence Parry Heide

Janet Hamm Needs a Date for the Dance

by Eve Bunting

BANTAM BOOKS
NEW YORK • TORONTO • LONDON • SYDNEY • AUCKLAND

RL4, and IL 9–12

This low-priced Bantam Book
has been completely reset in a type face
designed for easy reading, and was printed
from new plates. It contains the complete
text of the original hard-cover edition.
NOT ONE WORD HAS BEEN OMITTED.

JANET HAMM NEEDS A DATE FOR THE DANCE

A Bantam Book / published by arrangement with
Houghton Mifflin Company

PRINTING HISTORY
Houghton Mifflin edition published March 1986
Bantam edition / July 1987

ISBN 0-553-15537-7

Published simultaneously in the United States and Canada

PRINTED IN THE UNITED STATES OF AMERICA

CW   0 9 8 7

To Dianne Canning with love
Special thanks to Lori Fry

Chapter One

All the seventh graders knew there was going to be an end-of-the-year dance. We just didn't know the details.

Karen and Star and I saw the first notice on the bulletin board on Tuesday, after school. We'd been to the library to return books, so we were late and most of the kids had already gone home. Only Danny De-Puzo stood in front of the bulletin board, and it was his voice that stopped us.

"Oh, look!" he said, in this fake whine he uses when he's trying to imitate a girl. "Here's the notice about the dance."

Karen sighed and pretended to look around. She doesn't like Danny that much. Actually, nobody likes Danny that much.

"I could have sworn I heard another girl somewhere," Karen said. "But there's only you and Star and me. Do you see anyone else, Janet?"

"Only crazy old Danny DePuzo," I said.

Danny gave a fake shriek. He thinks it's superfunny when he acts the way he thinks girls act. Danny has to be really dumb. Either he's putting girls down or trying to get one to go out with him. He never seems to understand that the two things don't go together.

"Oh, isn't this exciting!" Danny clutched at what I guess was his heart.

"SEVENTH GRADERS ... MARK YOUR CALENDARS," HE READ. "THE LEADERSHIP CLASS ANNOUNCES AN ALL SEVENTH GRADE DANCE TO BE HELD IN THE AUDITORIUM ON FRIDAY NIGHT, JUNE 8."

"Crumbs!" I said. "That's less than two weeks away. Shove over Danny and let *us* have a look."

Danny didn't move. "AND THIS YEAR," he read, ". . . THIS YEAR THE THEME WILL BE THE FIFTIES. SO START HITTING UP YOUR MOMS, DADS AND NEIGHBORS FOR ALL THOSE NIFTY FIFTIES' OUTFITS GATHERING MOTHS IN THEIR CLOSETS."

"Oh, oh," Danny staggered backward with his arms outstretched. "I can hardly stand it. We get to wear nifty fifties' stuff."

"We can hardly stand you," Karen said coldly.

I was about to add my insult to hers, but the words got stuck in my throat. Because I'd managed to push in next to Danny and my eyes had skimmed past the price of the tickets, etc., to the awful part that was tacked on at the end, like a rattle on a snake's tail.

"AND FOR THIS, THE VERY LAST DANCE OF THE SCHOOL YEAR, *DATING IS ACCEPTABLE.*"

Dating is acceptable? Oh, horrors! My mind slithered in a panic. Having to wait and wait and hope and hope that someone would ask you to go. Or worse yet, having to ask someone yourself and maybe having him say no. Who had decided THIS was acceptable? There was more, and I made myself go on reading. "NON-DATING IS EQUALLY ACCEPTABLE. WE WANT YOU THERE, WITH OR WITHOUT A PARTNER, BECAUSE THIS IS GOING TO BE THE BIGGEST SHINDIG ROOSEVELT JUNIOR HIGH HAS EVER HAD. WE'LL SHOW THOSE EIGHTH AND NINTH GRADERS HOW TO PUT ON A DANCE."

Danny had reached the "dating is acceptable" part now, and his voice had stopped being twittery.

"All right!" he said. He stuck his thumbs in the waist band of his jeans and turned around, giving us his famous DePuzo sexy look. Danny is the seventh grade sex fiend, no question.

Francine Grady had come up behind us and was reading about the dance too, and Danny included her in his leering look.

"So, let's see," he said. "First come, first served. Star? Want to go to the dance with me?"

Now we were all looking at Star. Face it, we're usually all looking at Star. Star is the prettiest girl in the whole school, and it's actually an honor to have her in the seventh grade. It gives us a lot of style.

Star has long, blond hair, violet eyes and dimples. She also has a cute figure, semiskinny, not semifat like mine. Not much *wonder* she was the first one to be asked to the dance.

"All the guys are going to want to take Star, you bozo," Francine Grady said. Francine is not far behind me in total truthfulness, though usually she's not so quick to admit how popular Star is.

Star's cheeks got pink, which made her look even prettier. When *mine* get pink, I look ready to explode.

"All the boys may want to *go* with Star," Danny drawled. I swear he practices that drawl in the shower! "But who does STAR want to go with? That's the important question."

It's hard to believe Danny would think she'd want to go with HIM. But with Danny you can believe anything.

"I'm a great dancer," he said, and I looked at him hard, because for a minute he sounded almost pleading. No! Couldn't be!

"I bet you are," Star said. "It's just . . . John and I have been talking a lot about the dance, and we sort of planned that we'd be together, and . . ." By John she meant John Hunt, who is her boyfriend, and when she said his name her cheeks got pinker than ever.

"No problem," Danny said. "You can GO with me

and dance as many times as you like with John. That'll be okay."

"I don't think that would work, Danny," Star said. "But thanks anyway."

Another thing about Star is, she's really nice. I had a hard time getting used to that when she first came to Roosevelt earlier this year. You just *expect* someone who looks that great to be a pain, and conceited and stuck up. Star isn't. Which makes me feel bad about myself when I wish she'd never come to our school. And I wish that a lot.

Danny was shrugging his shoulders now to show that it was all right with him if Star wanted to miss out on the chance of a lifetime.

I stood watching his eyes move around the rest of us, and I knew I was hoping he'd ask *me*. Horrors! What was the matter with me? Wanting rotten old Danny DePuzo to take me to the dance? But I knew why. It was because of that sick, fluttery feeling inside, that total FEAR that *nobody* would ask me.

I hummed a little and turned my back, pretending to read the other notices on the bulletin board, and I heard Danny say, "Karen? Karen Kepplewhite? How about it? I know you've learned to KISS really well. If you come with me, you'll learn to DANCE really well too. You'll just be an expert on everything."

"I already know how to dance, Danny, thank you very much," Karen said stiffly.

Karen is my best friend. Or she was, till Star came. Now I'm not sure. For her thirteenth birthday I gave her a book called *How to Kiss Like an Expert,* and Danny never quits teasing about it. Karen and I happen to know he bought a copy of the book for himself and read it secretly. He never admits it, of course.

"You'll be going with Mark, Karen, won't you?" Star asked.

Karen began picking at the corner of her English lit book, which was on the top of the pile she was carrying. When Karen picks like that, it's a definite sign she's nervous. "I don't know for sure," she said.

Man, this dating for the dance business was making *everyone* nervous. Even Karen, who knew perfectly well Mark Ritchie liked her and would ask her to the dance. Lucky Karen!

"If you don't know for sure, you'd better come with me," Danny said. "Mine is a sensational, never-to-be-repeated offer."

"No thanks, Danny," Karen said.

I went back to nonchalantly studying the notice-board. I practice being nonchalant all the time because it does not come easily to me. Beside me, Francine was nonchalantly studying the notices too.

I hummed my little tune to show how truly nonchalant I really was, and I thought, How awful to *ask* and be turned *down*. Even if the person is nice about it, it's still awful. I would DIE. Poor Danny! If he asked me next, I'd say . . . well, I wouldn't jump at it, but I'd sort of hestitate and then say, "Okay, I guess," as if it really wasn't all that important. But oh, what a relief it would be to know I had a date and I didn't need to worry for the next two weeks!

I peered at Danny sideways.

He was gazing down the hall where Miss Newsome's class was coming out of the computer lab. Miss Newsome's classes are always late getting out because the kids like to hang around and play games on the computers.

"It says here you can go without a date," Star said. "That might be more fun anyway."

"Naw," Danny said. "All the good-looking girls are going to have dates. There'll only be dogs left in the dog pen." He tittered in his totally obnoxious way.

I stopped reading and swung around. To think that even for a *minute* I'd been sorry for this . . . this creep! That even for a minute I'd been hoping— Don't *think* about that, Janet. That is too humiliating.

"There are all kinds of dogs, Danny DePuzo," I said. "Girl dogs and boy dogs. *Anybody* can invite *anybody*. I bet you end up in the dog pen yourself. No offense."

Karen says the way I tack "no offense" on the end of an insult doesn't make it any better. She's probably right. But I don't care a twiddle if I offend Danny DePuzo or not.

"Yeah! Which girl do you think is going to be desperate enough to ask YOU?" Francine sounded so mad that I knew she was scared of not having a date too, and that she'd had hopes about Danny as humiliating as mine. That made me feel a little better about myself. But not much.

Danny held up a hand. "Cool it! Cool it! Danny DePuzo will be at the dance with a good-looking babe, never you fear."

"We are *girls*, Danny. Not *babes, dolls, chicks* or other assorted creatures," Karen said. "Is that so hard to remember?"

"Whatever." Danny hitched up his jeans and swaggered down the hall. I saw him stop partway along to talk to Connie Wu.

"If he's asking Connie, I hope she tells him to drop dead," Francine said. "I hope he asks a hundred girls, and they all tell him to drop dead." Francine has red hair and freckles and she can make her eyes into littler slits than anybody I've ever seen. We began walking down the hallway, away from that awful Danny De-Puzo, and that awful notice board.

"Are you going to invite someone, Janet?" Francine asked me.

"I haven't decided." It was weird the way Francine had put that. It was as if she already *knew* that nobody would ask me and that I'd have to be the one to do the asking. "Besides," I added nonchalantly, "Star *could* be right. It could be more fun going with a group."

"Yeah." Francine nodded. "Then we wouldn't be stuck with the same dumb guy all night."

I knew Francine would *love* to be stuck with the same guy all night. I knew I would too. We were both doing something here. It was like telling everyone when you come out of a math test that you KNOW you've failed. That way they're prepared for the big F, and you're prepared too. Nobody expects too much from you, and nobody's disappointed. Not even you.

Chapter Two

Karen and Star and I live close to each other, so we walk home together. It used to be just Karen and I before Star came. Actually, Star lives with her mother in the same apartment house as Karen's grandmother. So Star and Karen see each other a lot. Especially now, because Karen's parents are on vacation, and she and her little brother are staying with their gran.

"Can you *believe* that Danny DePuzo?" Karen asked.

"Can you believe I used to *like* him?" I asked. "That was when I was younger and totally *dumb*," I told Star, who was looking astonished. No point in admitting that I was talking about only a few months ago. I knew Karen wouldn't tell. "I used to think he had a great bod," I added.

"He does have a nice bod," Star agreed.

"Stinky personality though." Karen turned up her nose as if she smelled a bad smell.

Thank heavens neither of them knew what I'd been wishing!

It's funny what happens when you walk home as a threesome. Three don't fit across the sidewalk in some places. Usually one of us has to be in front. Usually it seems to be me. I hope that's because I walk faster. I began going backward so I could face them as I talked.

"Why do you think they decided to do it this way? I mean, having dating?"

"Oh, they're probably trying to *mature* us," Karen said. "It's so stupid." She picked at the corner of her English lit book again. "I guess it's okay if someone wants to go with you. Or if there's someone you want to take."

"You know Mark's going to ask you, Karen," I said. "For absolutely positively sure."

"I don't know for absolutely positively sure. Mark's shy. Maybe he won't even go. Remember, Janet? He almost didn't come to my birthday party because there were kissing games."

Karen's frightened eyes flickered toward me, and suddenly I didn't feel so bad. I mean, I want her to have a date for the dance, because she *is* my best friend. And it would be real mean of me if I didn't. But if *she* doesn't have a date and *I* don't have a date, then we could go together, and Star would be with John, and it would be the way it used to be.

"Karen?" Star said. "Why don't you call Mark and ask him? That would make it easier for him."

"Oh, I couldn't!" Karen looked at me to see if I understood.

Of course I understood. I'd been her best friend for years and years, hadn't I? Star had only known her for months. You can't totally understand a person in just months. I turned round and walked with my back toward them again, because my neck was hurting from looking two ways at once.

Behind me Star was asking, "Where can we get those fifties' dresses, or whatever they wore?"

"Maybe your mom has some," Karen said.

"No. We didn't bring that much stuff with us. Mom got rid of all her old things. She didn't want to keep remembering."

Karen was silent, and I was too. I knew we were both thinking how awful it must have been for Star and her mother when Star's dad died. I guess that's one reason why they decided to move from San Francisco.

I feel so guilty sometimes when I wish Star had never come to our town. In fact, I feel like a monster. And it doesn't help a bit when I tell myself that I'm only wishing her dad hadn't died. I do wish that, of course. It's just . . . Karen *really* likes Star. A whole bunch.

Karen was counting on her fingers. "Wait a sec. Our

moms are all too young anyway. They were all real little in the fifties. My mom wasn't born till 1951."

We walked quietly, considering the problem. Of course, I mightn't even *have* a problem. Not if I wasn't going to the dance. And if I didn't have a date, I wasn't. Imagine being in the *dog pen,* and having Danny De-Puzo smirking at you as he boogied past. And seeing Star dancing with John, and Karen dancing with Mark and having to go hide in the bathroom so they wouldn't know that none of the guys even liked you enough to ask you for *one dance.* Suddenly I felt weepy, and I grabbed my nose and gave a good, hard swallow, which is what I do at a sad movie if I don't want to cry. It stops the tears when they're only halfway to your eyes.

"I just wish Mickey Mouse hadn't moved away," Karen said suddenly.

I kept on walking, and Karen caught up and walked next to me. She probably knew how I was feeling. Sometimes we know that about each other.

"Michael really liked you, Jan," Star said.

I nodded and managed not to gulp. Mickey Mouse's real name is Michael Moss, and he'd almost been my boyfriend for three weeks. He'd taken me to the movies once and we'd held hands. But then his family moved away. His mom's an engineer, and she was transferred to Denver, Colorado. I don't think Michael could have liked me *that* much, though, because he never wrote once. Even though I sent him a card from the space museum.

"You know what I think?" Star said. "I think every-body'll be together anyway. It's not going to be boy/girl, boy/girl. You can be with us, Jan. I mean, if you decide not to go with anyone."

I gave Star a grateful smile over my shoulder. She really *is* nice. She's making it seem as if I'm going to have a choice!

"Wasn't that ghastly what Danny said about the dog pen?" I asked. That dog pen was DEFINITELY on my mind.

Karen nodded. "Danny's a rodent."

"Total," I agreed.

We'd come to Star's apartment building now, and we all stopped.

"Gran made tutti-frutti salad, and there's some left," Karen said. "Want to come up and have some, Jan?"

"I can't. I have piano. And I have to go home first and grab my music."

"Well come after, then. If it's okay with your mom," Karen said. "Star and I are teaching Gran how to knit. You can learn too, if you want."

"I don't want to learn how to knit," I said. "But I'll come over anyway."

"Great! We can talk about the dance. See you later."

I watched Karen and Star disappear through the swinging glass doors. Star said something, and Karen laughed. I could still see them as they climbed the stairs inside, and I felt like bawling again. Sometimes I don't know the reason I feel this way, and sometimes I do. And when I do it's even worse.

Nasty, jealous green-eyed cat
No one wants you here, so scat.

When I get jealous, I say this to myself inside my head. It's supposed to remind me to quit. "They asked you to come, too, dumbo," I muttered out loud. But Karen and Star had seemed so TOGETHER going up those stairs. I hoped they weren't saying "Poor Janet!" and stuff like that, now that they were by themselves.

My big brother, Wilmer, was rushing out of our door just as I was going in. He almost knocked me over.

"Hey, watch it!" I said.

"I'm late for D and D Club," he yelled over his shoulder. "I'm supposed to meet Colin."

D and D stands for Dungeons and Dragons, which is a terribly complicated fantasy game that some of the kids in high school play. Colin is Wilmer's friend from school who is also a D and D freak. I've never met him, but he's supposed to be someone real important in the club.

Wilmer was unlocking his bike. "She's on the phone again," he yelled. "Something's UP. U-P UP! And wait till you see inside. Boy, are you going to be knocked out!"

By *she,* Wilmer meant Mom. Because of the dance

and the dating scare I'd forgotten the new mystery about HER.

"She's met someone," Wilmer had said last night, nodding and looking very knowing.

"How *could* she have met someone?" I'd asked. "She never goes *out*."

"She never used to talk on the phone all the time either," he'd said. "She's not talking to herself!"

Mom was talking to someone now, all right. I could hear her the minute I opened the door. And the minute I opened the door I saw why Wilmer had said I'd be knocked out. The house was tidy. Not only tidy, but spiffy clean. I hadn't seen it like this since before Dad left, more than four years ago, and I couldn't remember that too well. It was too far back.

Mom was sitting in the corner of the couch beside the phone table. She was wearing nice white pants and a pale blue shirt and her hair was tied back with a blue ribbon. Mom, her hair tied back with a blue ribbon! It was enough to knock anybody out!

She waved to me and said into the phone, "Really? Oh, I'd love to." And then she giggled. No kidding! If I hadn't heard that giggle come out of my mother's mouth, I wouldn't have believed it.

I went in the kitchen, and I must say my ears were twitching, trying to hear more. There seemed to be only silence.

I grabbed a carrot from the crisper drawer and saw

that the refrigerator had been all cleaned out. Even the kitchen floor shone.

"Just a second," Mom said into the phone as I came back through the living room. She put her hand over the mouthpiece. "Penny called. She says she'll be a half hour late with your lesson."

Penny's my piano teacher.

"Okay," I said. "Is that Penny on the phone?"

"Penny? No." Mom smiled, and I swear she looked real pretty and young.

"I'm going to Karen's gran's afterward," I said.

"All right."

I noticed she didn't uncover the mouthpiece all the time she talked to me. I could hear her say something softly as I closed the front door behind me.

What if Wilmer's right? I thought as I walked to Penny's. What if she's met someone, and they fall in love and she marries him? It might be nice having a grown-up man around, even if he wasn't Dad. I'd given up on Dad anyway. The new man and Mom might be like Karen's parents, and they'd come to school for "hospitality night" and things like that. Maybe he'd be great. On the other hand, maybe he'd be a toad, and hate me, and think I was FAT. And UGLY. Why were there always two possibilities for everything? Such as . . . maybe someone would ask me to the dance and maybe someone wouldn't.

When I got to Penny's house, I heard someone inside playing the piano. It was still too early, so I sat in the swing Penny graciously provides on her front lawn under the California Live Oak. Whoever was playing was supergood, really advanced. I finished my carrot, then I dug a hole with my toe and planted the carrot top under Penny's hedge. It would be lovely for Penny to come out some morning and find she had a carrot tree right next to the Live Oak.

I did some lazy swinging. I decided that when I got back home I'd make a list of boys I'd *want* to ask to the dance, a list of boys I *could* ask and a list of the boys who might ask *me*. Unfortunately, I could only think of names for the first list.

A ginger-colored cat came sniffing at my carrot tree. I shooed him away, and then Penny's door opened and a kid of about eleven came out. He had neat, straight, black hair and shiny owl glasses. The glasses turned in my direction and then the boy marched off down the driveway.

Penny's cheery voice called from her porch. "Jan? I'm ready for you. Sorry you had to wait. I had a new student, and I had to fit him in."

"That's okay," I said. "I had a lot of thinking to do and swinging helps. You should rent out your swing to thinkers, Penny."

Penny grinned. She's pretty old but she has the best smile, and brown hair that's long enough for her to sit on. "You can use the swing for free anytime, my friend," she said.

As soon as I sat at the piano, she said, "Let's start with your choice, Jan."

Penny always lets us start with whatever we like to put us in the mood before we get down to business. I thought for a couple of seconds and then began on *Yesterday, all my troubles seemed so far away.*

"Nice," Penny said when I finished. "You really played that with a lot of feeling, Janet."

I sighed. She was right. That was how I'd played it all right.

Chapter Three

Karen's gran's name is Kepplewhite too. DEIRDRE
KEPPLEWHITE is printed on a card by her apartment
door. I'd just about touched the bell when Georgie,
Karen's little brother, flung open the door. He was
wearing a black knitted cap, a black cape and eyeglasses
without glass.

"Who are *you?*" I asked.

"I am Lord of the Dark Moon Planet."

"Oh."

"It's okay," he whispered, pulling off the glasses. "I'm
REALLY Georgie."

"Whew! You scared me there." I wiped my brow.

"*They're* knitting," Georgie said in a disgusted voice
and jerked a thumb over his shoulder.

They sure were. Knitting and sitting together, the three of them on the couch.

Karen's gran darted a quick glance at me and an even quicker one back at her knitting. "Hi, Janet."

Star and Karen said "Hi" too and then Star said, "You can't just ignore stitches when you drop them, Mrs. Kepplewhite. You have to pick them up again. Here, I'll do it for you."

I stood watching them, feeling left out again. The thing is, I was dying to talk to Karen about maybe not going to the dance, and about my mom and the mysterious phone calls. If Karen had been here just with her gran I'd have sat down and told them *both*, because Mrs. Kepplewhite is okay, and she usually has good stuff to say. Or else Karen and I would have gone in the kitchen and whispered. But since Star's come, everything's changed. She's always around, and I'm still not that sure about her.

Georgie was tugging at my arm. "Want to hear me play my flute?"

"Janet does not want to hear you play your flute, Georgie," Karen said.

But he was already tooting away on a plastic whistle that had only one note.

Karen gave me a pained look. "It was in the Fruit Crackles box this morning. Imagine if he'd swallowed it! He'd have been tooting all over the house."

"Especially when we squeezed him," Star said.

"I don't ever let you squeeze me," Georgie began in a high voice, but Mrs. Kepplewhite interrupted. She's very good at interrupting at the right time.

"Janet might like to see your new maze, Georgie." She gasped. "Oops, I just dropped another stitch."

I don't truly know why Mrs. Kepplewhite's learning to knit. I mean, if you haven't needed to knit for seventy-five years, why start now? But that's the way she is. She learned to play tennis a while back, and she was in a class with all ten-year-olds. This year she worked for months solving a Rubik's Cube. She's so proud of it that now she keeps it up on the mantle under a plastic dome. I guess whatever she's knitting will end up on the mantel too.

"Want to see my maze?" Georgie dragged me across to the dining-room table. Georgie loves mazes. I looked at this one, all scrawled over like a spider's web and said, "*Good,* Georgie." Georgie never bothers with the paths. He just takes a red crayon and starts at the edge of the page and wanders all over the place. Sometimes he gives me a different color, and I add another web on top of his.

I was just about to grab a green Crayola when the phone in the kitchen rang. Georgie was off like a lightning bolt.

"Kepplewhite residence," he piped.

The knitters waited, needles stilled.

"It's for you, Karen," Georgie called. "It's Mark-eeeee. Mark-eeeee." He screeched the name at the top of his lung power, and I swear if he'd been my little brother I would have *killed* him.

Karen threw down her knitting. Her face was really red and she said, "Georgie! You're going to get it! Gran, tell him—"

"It has to be about the dance, Karen," Star whispered. Her face was pink too. It wasn't hard to see she was happy for Karen. Well, I was too, of course.

Mrs. Kepplewhite's apartment isn't very big, since usually she's the only one who lives in it. She has a phone in the kitchen and another in the bedroom.

"You can go in my room and close the door, Karen," she said.

Karen gave Georgie another glare. "Jan? Hang up for me in the kitchen, will you? And don't let the pest listen in."

I glared at the pest too. "He'd better not try."

I had to listen myself for a couple of seconds, to make sure Karen had picked up the phone. I listened just long enough to hear Mark say, in his nice, shy voice, "Karen? This is Mark."

Of course it was Mark. As if everyone from here to Glendale hadn't heard Georgie *shouting* who it was. I hung the phone up quietly and stood staring at it. Just about now he'd be asking her to go to the dance. And just about now she'd be saying yes.

"Janet?" Georgie pulled at my T-shirt. "What are you looking at, Janet?"

"The phone."

"What's the matter with it?"

"Nothing."

"Are you mad at me for yelling *Mark-eeee* like that?"

"No. But Karen is. You heard her. You're going to get it."

I swear, that little Georgie's the cutest thing, especially when he's done something bad and he's a little scared. He looked up at me through his silly no-glass glasses. His eyes are a real dark brown, and he has lashes so long you could trip over them. It gives Karen a fit since hers are of the semi-stubby variety. No offense.

Georgie also has the kind of skin you see on baby dolls, so smooth it's unreal. Karen comforts herself that he'll get zits like everyone else when he's older. Sometimes he's so cute I get these uncontrollable urges to hug him, especially when I'm a little sad, like now. But Georgie isn't into hugging. Usually I just grab him around the stomach and turn him upside down instead, which he loves. I picked him up now, stood him on his head and listened to him giggle.

"Hey, Georgie, you're sure cute," I said. "You want to take me to the dance?"

His cloak had fallen forward over his head, muffling his words. "Uh-uh. No way."

I jiggled him a bit, and his glasses came off. "Going to take me to the dance? We'll have fun. We can dance with you upside down like this if you want."

"No. No." Georgie raised his voice. "Gran help!"

I jiggled some more. He was pawing at his Lord of the Dark Moon Planet cloak and trying to wriggle free, but I had a good grip.

"Let me up, Janet."

"Not until you say you'll go to the dance with me."

"Okay. I'll go. Let me up, I'm getting sick."

I stood him upright. His eyes were glazed, and he wobbled a bit. Maybe I *had* held him too long. "Hey, Georgie Porgie! I'm sorry. I was only kidding around. I didn't mean to . . ."

Georgie found his glasses and put them on. He gave me a wobbly grin. "That was fun."

"Want some more?" I lunged toward him, and he stepped back.

"No way!" His voice was getting higher, and I could tell he'd decided to be mad. "And I'm not going to that stupid dance with you either. I wouldn't go to that stupid dance with you if you were . . . if you were . . . if you were Princess Leia."

"Princess Leia from *Star Wars*? And *The Empire Strikes Back*? You'd go with me, Georgie. You *love* Princess Leia."

"Well, I wouldn't, not even if you were her." He sailed out of the kitchen, and his voice floated back to me. "And you can't play with my maze anymore either."

"Janet?" Karen was standing in the kitchen door. Her face was the same color Georgie's had been, and she hadn't even been standing on her head.

"Mark asked you to the dance?" I tried to sound excited for her. I really did.

She nodded, and I nodded too. "That's great, Karen."

She went ahead of me into the living room, and the minute Star saw her she stood up and they hugged each other and hopped around. Karen and I used to do that a lot. Like when Michael Moss asked me out. And when we both made it into the chorale in sixth grade. I wished I'd hugged her when she came into the kitchen.

Georgie glared at me from his place at the table. "Mean old Janet isn't going," he said.

Karen's gran put down her knitting. "Who wants tutti-frutti?"

"Oh yes, in just a second." Karen plopped down on the couch and kicked her legs in the air.

"It's so great that you know, Karen," Star said. "Now we can . . ." She stopped. And I knew why she'd stopped. Karen had given her a meaningful look.

I recognize meaningful looks. Actually, I *invented* them between Karen and me. I knew *exactly* what that meaningful look said. It said, Stop! Janet's here. And she's not supposed to know. It's *our* secret.

There was a throbbing kind of silence. How awful! Karen and Star had a secret.

Georgie's whistle was on the table, and I grabbed it and began to toot. He jumped up and tried to get it away from me. "Give me back my flute. You can't play on it, either," he said.

I held it up out of his reach. A secret. A secret about the dance.

"You're so mean, Janet!" Georgie said. "Nobody would want to go to the dance with a mean, terrible girl like you."

I decided Georgie was probably right.

Chapter Four

The next morning started off ordinary enough.

Wilmer was in the kitchen fixing himself one of his gross blender drinks that has yogurt, and raw eggs, and wheat germ in it.

"Want some?" He gave me a quick wiggle of his eyebrows.

"Uh-uh." I poured cereal and peeled myself a banana. Maybe I'd pretend to be sick today and not even *go* to school. All that *dance* talk! Who needed it? Maybe I'd still be sick the night of the dance.

Mom was in the shower upstairs. I could hear the water running.

"She was talking on the phone again last night when I came back from D and D Club," Wilmer said. "In her bedroom."

"Don't call her *she*," Dad used to say. "You are speaking of your mother. Show some respect." And then he'd walked out on her, which wasn't a bit respectful.

Wilmer sat on the countertop and drank straight from the glass container. Almost half of his yucky drink disappeared in a few swallows. He wiped his mouth and thumped the pitcher down. "Do you know how I know she was talking on the phone in her bedroom?"

I sprinkled substitute sugar on my cereal.

"That stuff kills rats," Wilmer said.

I ignored him. "I guess you heard her talking," I said.

"I heard all right. I listened in."

"What?" I stopped slicing my banana.

"I came in late and I picked up the phone to call Colin. He's Dungeon Master in the club, and I forgot to tell him something. Anyway, Mom was on the phone, gabbing away to this new guy."

I went back to slicing. "And . . . ?"

"And he was asking her if she'd like to go to Tahiti with him and telling her how they'd run together on the sands at sunset. He has this real mellow voice."

I stopped again. "Are you sure he said Tahiti and not *Hawaii?*"

"Oh for Pete's sake, Janet, what's the difference? This was a guy. Asking our mom to run away with him."

"It's just . . . Tahiti's so far. I thought maybe you'd made a mistake. Who *is* this guy, anyway? Is he going to marry her first, or what? Did she say she'd go?"

Something cold was spreading inside of me, and it wasn't my cereal. I hadn't even started on that yet. "Did she say she'd *go,* Wilmer?"

"She laughed and said 'Don't you think we ought to know each other a little better first?'"

"And what did he say?"

"He hardly let her finish, he was so busy telling her about this little hotel on the beach and how—"

"Wait a sec. You listened to all that? What a toadface! That's *eavesdropping!* That stuff sounds *private.*"

"It *was* private." Wilmer finished off what was left in the blender. "But you and I need to know, don't we?"

I picked up my half banana and studied it carefully. The black in the middle looked like a worm, a great, long worm that started at one end and went to the other. All those little pieces of sliced worm were lying in my cereal bowl. "Are you sure it wasn't Dad?"

"It wasn't Dad. Shh! Here she comes."

Mom was dressed already in the blue shirtwaist dress that I like and that she hasn't worn in ages because it has to be ironed. She must have ironed it yesterday. I wondered if she was planning that trip to Tahiti. I wondered if she'd give us some warning before she left or just disappear one day the way Dad did.

"Mom?" Wilmer asked. "Is it okay if I bring a friend home from school today? We're in D and D. We thought we'd have a short session here, today and to-morrow, if that's all right."

"Sure." Mom didn't even blink. You would think

that Wilmer asking to bring someone home was the most normal thing in the world. Which it isn't. I don't know *when* he last brought someone here. Or when I did. Face it, when the house is a total mess, and your mom is too, it's not easy. You have to be pretty sure of yourself *and* your friends before you invite them over.

"Great," Wilmer said. He rinsed out the blender, then bent over to tug my hair. "See you, toots."

Sometimes, when Wilmer's in a good mood, he calls me *toots,* which is probably sexist. But maybe not if it's coming from your brother.

With all the talking, I was late, and I had to dash to school. Karen and I have an arrangement that if I'm not at her house by eight, she goes on without me. This morning I couldn't be at her gran's in time, so I guess she went on. With Star.

I'd known all the talk in school would be about the dance and it was. Who was going with what guy. Who had hopes. Well, face it, just about everyone had HOPES. Which girl was revving up her courage to ask which guy. I tried to be *very* nonchalant.

Karen and Star and I were standing outside homeroom when Francine Grady came puffing up. Star was looking adorable, as usual. She had on her pink pleated skirt and the cotton turtleneck with the baby-pink elephants on it.

Karen looked really nice too. I don't know if Karen's prettier than she was before she started playing tennis and going ice skating and stuff with Mark. It doesn't seem possible, but I swear she is. Maybe having a boy-friend makes a person prettier.

I'd decided to act as usual with her and Star, and try not to think about the secret. I definitely was *not* going to HINT or BEG to find out.

"Guess what?" Francine said as she slid to a stop beside us.

Her "guess what" was so triumphant that I knew "what" before she told us. In the loudest imaginable voice, she said, "*I've* got a date for the dance!"

"You don't have to shout, Francine!" I covered my ears. "No offense."

"No offense yourself, Janet Hamm. You'd probably tell the world if you had a date. You'd probably PAY somebody to write it in the sky." She turned so she was talking only to Karen and Star, sort of putting me in my place. "His name's Chance Matthews, and he's OLDER."

"You mean he's your uncle or something?" I asked.

Francine gave me an ugly look, then smiled at Star. "Isn't that the most fantastic name you ever heard in your whole life? Chance! Doesn't it make you think of a cowboy? The Marlboro man, riding in his horse on the snow?"

"Shouldn't it be riding *on* his horse *in* the snow?" I asked, but Francine ignored me.

Danny DePuzo had come sneaking up behind us in his usual frog-toed way, and I guess he'd been listening.

"The guy's taking some CHANCE with you, Francine." He dug an elbow in my ribs. "Get it, Janet? Chance? Chance?"

I moved a step away. "Quit it, Danny."

Francine's eyes slid from Danny to me. "I'll tell you one thing. *I* won't be in the dog pen."

Star spoke quickly. "Did you have to get permission to bring him, Francine? I thought only seventh graders could go."

Francine tossed her hair. "Oh, I just talked with Miss Wilson in the office. She's going to let me know. But she's sure it will be okay. Chance says they can call his mother."

"His *mother?*" Even *I* was impressed.

"How old is this guy, anyway?" Danny asked.

"He's in ninth grade at Poly, if you must know, Danny DePuzo. And he's really cool." Francine turned back to Karen and Star. "You know how neat Poly guys are. As soon as I said the magic word, Miss Wilson softened up. 'Oh he's from POLY,' she said. 'He must be really smart!'"

Danny's glance shifted to me. "Well, I guess that only leaves Janet. I'll pass the word."

Simon Wuhlfeiler was going by, his head buried in a book as usual. Danny raised his voice. "Hey, Simon! Janet Hamm needs a date for the dance. Pass the word."

I almost fainted. Truly, I could feel weakness coming. Fortunately Danny had picked a good person to shout at, because Simon is out in space somewhere and hears nothing. He just looked up and then back at his book.

"You shut up this minute, Danny," Karen said fiercely. "Janet does *not* need a date. She's coming with us."

"Besides, it's ages yet till the dance," Star said. "You don't know what's going to happen."

My weakness was subsiding. I don't know what made me say what I said next. It might have been Danny's smirky face or Francine's uppity smile. Or even Karen and Star being so nice . . . but so uppity in a way themselves. So sure *they* were going to have to take me with them. The words just popped out of my mouth.

"Janet Hamm does *not* need a date for the dance. Janet Hamm *has* a date for the dance."

"Janet!" Karen gasped. "How great! How come you didn't tell us?"

"I didn't have a chance with Francine and everybody talking."

Danny's eyes widened. "Somebody *asked* you?" Oh, that Danny DePuzo! And to think I once liked his bod.

"If you must know," I said, imitating Francine, "*I* asked somebody. And the somebody said yes." No need to tell them the somebody was five years old and that I'd been holding him upside down at the time. And that afterwards he'd said he wouldn't go with me, not even if I were Princess Leia.

"Well, who is it?" Francine stared at me with slitty, suspicious eyes.

I twirled the ends of my hair the way she does and tried for my nonchalant look. "A boy."

"We know that. Which boy?" Francine was not going to be put off.

"You don't even know him, Francine," I said, changing from nonchalant to cold.

"But you're going to tell us, aren't you?" Karen asked.

By *us*, she meant her and Star. When Karen said "us" like that, and she didn't mean her and me, it made me feel bad. I examined my nails. I *would* tell them later, of course, because this was only a joke. A joke on Danny and Francine. But she and Star had kept a secret from me. They could wait.

"Does he go to Poly?" Francine asked. I thought she sounded kind of nervous.

"Uh-uh." I had a hard time not giggling. What if I said: "He goes to Sunnyside Nursery School." I didn't, of course.

"Well, you're going to need special permission too." Francine looked a little shocked, as though I'd stolen some of her triumph. I almost giggled again. Imagine Georgie in his glassless glasses and his Lord of the Dark Moon Planet cape standing in front of Miss Wilson, holding my hand.

"May I have permission to take Georgie as my date?" I'd say and she'd peer down and down and down.

"*I* told about Chance," Francine said. "It's no fair if you don't tell."

"I *know* you told, Francine. You told the whole world. I like to keep stuff like this private!"

"Oh la-di-da!" Francine went all slitty-eyed again.

Danny DePuzo had been studying me carefully. "You're making him up," he said. "There isn't anybody."

"Oh, yes, there is." I kept my eyes glued to his. That's a sure way to convince people you're telling the truth, which I was.

"Do you swear?" Danny asked.

"I swear."

"Janet does not tell lies," Karen said. Which is true, too.

They were all looking at me, and I could see Danny trying to find a loophole somewhere so he could stick my head in it.

"It's your uncle," he said.

I shook my head. "No relative."

Danny lifted his right hand. "You *swear* you asked a boy to go with you to the dance at Roosevelt, and you swear he said yes?"

I lifted my hand too. "I swear."

"Well, all I can say then is, the world is full of weird-os," Danny said.

Karen sniffed. "You should know, Danny DePuzo."

Francine played with one of her earrings. She got her ears pierced last summer, and she has a real earring wardrobe. These ones had little happy dangling faces, and I have to admit they were darling.

"I guess we'll have to be patient and wait to see what Janet produces." Francine sounded as if it would be no surprise to her if I came to the dance with a full-grown baboon. "I *bet* he's not as cute as Chance," she said.

I smirked. "Cuter. Actually, he's just about the cutest boy I've ever seen."

I felt great as I looked around at all their faces. They hadn't thought I could get a date, and I had. I'd fooled them. Suddenly reality set in like someone hitting me on the head with a water balloon. I'd fooled them all. But somewhere along the way this had gone too far. Although I hadn't lied once, I was beginning to feel that I had. And how was I going to get out of it?

Chapter Five

I didn't want Karen and Star quizzing me on the way home, so as soon as my last class was over, I split fast. And I went the long way home so they wouldn't catch up. It sure was *different* trying to dodge Karen and Star. Actually, it would have been a relief to tell them. And in a way I wanted to. But in a way I didn't.

I remembered things. The way they'd hugged each other. My left-out feeling. Well, now I was IN. I was *one of them* again. I was EQUAL. They could hug me, too. I remembered their secret look. They could keep that because now I had my own secret. Man, did I *ever!* One I wasn't too happy about.

When I go the long way home, I pass Penny's house. The swing was empty this afternoon. Inside, someone trailed a scale up and down the piano keys. I went across the yard and examined my carrot tree, which looked slightly droopy.

Penny has a big glass bottle of drinking water on her porch and a stack of pull-out paper cups. I put down my book bag and gave the carrot tree three cups of water before I got on the swing.

A hummingbird with a red breast and a green back darted from the Live Oak to Penny's feeder. It drank, gargled, drank and zoomed away. A giant bee buzzed around the marigolds. I closed my eyes, swung, and tried to think.

When someone spoke behind me, I almost fell off the swing.

"Want a push?" a voice asked.

I quickly spun me and the swing around. It was the kid from yesterday, the one with the owl glasses. He was wearing the kind of khaki shorts that have a zillion pockets. I think they're the kind you buy for a jungle expedition. His white knit tennis shirt had an alligator on the pocket. Under his arm was his music.

"Help!" I said. "You really scared me. Where did you come from?"

"I was sitting on the grass at the side of the porch."

"You should try the swing when you have to wait," I told him. "It's nice."

The boy nodded toward the carrot tree. "There's no point in watering that. Someone just stuck it in there."

"I did."

"Oh." He waited a few seconds then said, "Do you want a push?"

"No thanks. I hate to go high." I jumped off. When I stood beside the boy, I could see the top of his head. "How come you're having another lesson today?"

"I have a recital," he said. "Penny's working with me."

"A recital? Boy!" The kid must be a musical genius. I didn't know what else to say. "I'm Janet."

"I know. Penny told me. You go to Roosevelt. I'm Rolf."

"Rolf?" I sounded like a puppy barking, and I quick tried to cover it up by faking a cough.

"Rolf's a terrible name," he said. "It's German."

"It's probably real nice in German," I told him. "Anyway, you can't help names." I had the urge to pat him on the top of his silky, shiny black head the way I pat Georgie. "My last name's *Hamm*. How would you like to be called THAT? Especially when . . . well, I'm not *fat* exactly. But close enough for jokes."

"I don't think you're fat at all," Rolf said.

"Thanks. Did you just come to Pasadena?"

"Yeah. My dad's an engineer at Jacobs. He was transferred."

"I know about engineers getting transferred," I said gloomily. "If Mickey Mouse's mother hadn't had to go to Denver, I wouldn't have been in all this trouble."

Rolf was looking at me with polite interest, which was nice since he didn't know Mickey Mouse was really

Michael Moss. He must have thought I was slightly nutty, though.

"I have to go," I said.

Rolf called after me. "Janet? Carrots would be nice in there. If you like, I'll ask Penny if it's okay, and I'll buy some carrot seeds. We could plant them on Tuesday, after your lesson. I bet they have seed packages in the market."

"That's okay," I said. "But thanks anyway."

I got my book bag and went slowly home. Rolf seemed like a nice kid. But who needed a carrot garden? I mean, my life was complicated enough already.

When I opened our front door, I half expected Mom to be sitting on the couch with the phone glued to her ear. But she wasn't in the living room at all. Everything was clean and shiny. Even today's paper was neatly folded. I breathed in a smell of lemon or gardenia or something. Furniture polish, maybe. Wonderful! Except maybe she'd cleaned it all up for HIM, the guy with the mellow voice. Maybe he was coming over to be introduced. Horrors!

I heard talking in the dining room and remembered that Wilmer was bringing a friend home that afternoon.

"Wilmer? Where's Mom?" Suddenly I had that *cold* feeling again.

"She's not here," Wilmer yelled.

I moved slowly toward the dining room. "She didn't go to Tahiti already . . . ?" I began.

Wilmer was sitting at the table. He looked up and grinned. "Naw. She left a note in the kitchen. She's only at the market."

The other guy, who'd had his back to me, turned and smiled.

"This is Colin O'Malley. Colin, this is my sister, Janet."

I stared.

You know those games you play where you make up "the boy you'd most like to date"? You say, "He'll have Michael Jackson's eyes. And John Travolta's chin. And Bruce Springsteen's ears." I always go for Bruce Springsteen's ears. They're just about perfect.

Well, Colin was the perfect date in person. He had curly black hair, a pointy chin and really tanned skin. His nose was a teeny bit too long—just a teeny bit though. I decided he was supernice looking. *Mature* looking. And he was my brother Wilmer's *friend!* If I'd known Wilmer had a friend like this, I'd have been nicer to him all these years.

I held on to the edge of the table and said "hi" in my most nonchalant manner.

"Hi," Colin said.

When Wilmer talks about D and D Club and Dungeons and Dragons, I never pay any attention. All of a sudden I was fascinated. I gazed down at the big vinyl cloth that was spread on the table between them. There were trails drawn on it with marker pen and four little figures stood stiffly here and there. Scattered about were small squares of cardboard and different-looking dice. It wasn't hard to tell that this was a super brainy kind of game.

"I've *always* wanted to learn how to play this," I said. "Is it hard?"

Wilmer gathered up a couple of the dice. "You've always wanted to learn? That's news to me."

"Maybe I haven't said." I gave him a warning look. "How does it work, exactly?"

Colin smiled. He had a wide mouth. Sensitive, I decided.

"Do you have a couple of months?" he asked. He picked up one of the little figures. "Well, this is my character—Alaric, the Paladin."

I leaned closer. The figure was a shining knight with sword upraised. It looked so noble, so stern, so perfect for him.

"Wow!" I murmured.

He picked up a second. "Here's another of my characters. The cleric. I can cleanse anything that's unholy, drive out demons. Just ask."

"How come you're two people?" I hoped that was an intelligent question.

"It's a tough world out there," Colin said. "There are trolls to fight and dragons to slay. One character can't handle it all."

He was right about it being a tough world. And I

hadn't met up with any trolls or dragons yet. Not unless you counted Danny DePuzo. "Are these other two characters yours, Wilmer?" I asked.

"Yep. Fighter and Magic User."

I bent over to pick up one of the pieces of cardboard.

"Watch it!" Colin warned. "That's a dragon."

In his I'm-making-an-effort-to-be-patient voice, Wilmer said, "Do you mind, Janet? We're trying to play a game here."

"Okay, okay." I moved slowly from the table to the living-room couch and picked up Mom's little phone book. It has a black plastic cover. I discovered I could half open the book, hold it up as if I were reading, and still see on either side. I could see all of Colin's back except for an inch or two in the middle.

I wasn't paying any attention to the book itself. But suddenly something zinged from the page into my brain. A number had been written, right on the first page. Around it were a bunch of penciled hearts, hearts around hearts around hearts, like little valentine boxes fitted together.

Mom doodling *hearts*? It had to be the mystery guy's phone number, and it was beginning to blur a bit in front of my eyes. I sat, looking at the number, still aware of Colin and Wilmer at the table, but concentrating on these figures. I didn't know why. It was as if I were trying to memorize them.

There was no sound in either of the two rooms except the snap as Wilmer cracked his knuckles. He does that when he's thinking hard, or when he's worried or embarrassed. It's very aggravating.

I was still studying that number. I don't know why I copied it onto the pad by the phone, or why I ripped the page from the pad and put it in my pocket. I wasn't going to *call* this guy or anything. It was just some kind of link, one small piece of knowing, a start on a trail that could be followed if Mom did, by any chance, disappear to Tahiti.

"Can't you find something to do someplace else?" Wilmer asked, and his knuckles went snap, crackle, pop. "Don't you have to practice piano?"

"You want me to practice *here? Now?*"

"On second thought," Wilmer said. "Why don't you go up to your room and practice reading?"

Sometimes Wilmer gives me a rash.

Chapter Six

Karen and Star and I walked home from school together the next afternoon.

"You want a clue to my mystery date?" I murmured, glancing sideways at them. "Let's see now! A clue, a clue!"

I couldn't remember ever having had as great a day. Even Danny DePuzo had been semirespectful. I loved the way Karen and Star had been buzzing around me all day. I loved the way they were hanging on my words now.

"A clue?" I said again, trying to visualize Georgie. "He's got the biggest brownest eyes you've ever seen," I said.

"Mmm!" Karen pretended to faint. "I *adore* boys

with brown eyes. Second best to blue." Mark Ritchie
has blue eyes.

"What else?" Star asked. "Does he play baseball, or
anything?"

I thought about Georgie, and how he and his dad
play catch at the front of their house all the time. Georgie misses almost every ball, which is pretty easy to do
when your baseball cap keeps slipping over your eyes.

"He *does* play baseball," I said, trying not to laugh.
"But he's not *terribly* athletic. He's more into reading. . . ."

Or being read to, I thought. Anything about space-
men. I remembered the maze books. "He's quite good
at the kind of games you play indoors."

"You mean Trivial Pursuit? Or chess?"

"That kind of thing," I said. Georgie is actually very
big on Chutes and Ladders. I know, because I've played
it with him plenty. He cheats and so does his gran.

Star sighed. "He sounds heavenly. Is he nice, too,
Janet? I mean, it's okay to be cute and smart, but if he's
horrible . . ."

"Really!" Karen shuddered. "Think of Danny De-
Puzo!"

"This boy is *very* nice." All at once I remembered the
flute. "He's sort of a musician, too." Wow! When Georgie grew up, he was going to be a great boyfriend for
someone. When you put all his good points together
like this, you could sure see his *potential*.

"You are absolutely driving us crazy," Karen said. "You're not going to keep him hidden till the very night of the dance, are you?"

Oh crumbs! This was all a lot of fun, but I shouldn't go on and on about it. It was such a temptation though. Maybe I'd just keep it up a little bit more and *bask* in it while it lasted. Before we got home today, I'd confess. I'd say, "Guess what, you guys? It was all a joke. And you won't believe who I was describing all the time!"

Suddenly I realized something. There still wasn't room for three of us across the sidewalk, but we seemed to be taking turns today, walking in front. I wasn't always the one left out. That was because I'd become the most interesting one. The most important. I couldn't get over it. It was hard to believe a date for the dance could do all this.

We'd stopped for a red light at the corner of Del Mar and California.

"No, he's not very tall," I was telling Karen. "I mean, he's not gigantically *huge,* but he's not a dwarf or anything. He's definitely still growing and probably—" I stopped.

Something made me look to my left, and there was Colin O'Malley, on his ten-speed, waiting for the light to change too.

Sometimes I think I have laser eyes. I didn't call his name or anything, but my stare must have burned right into his brain. He looked across at the three of us, puzzled, and then he saw me. For an awful second, I knew he didn't remember me. Now, that's *truly* humiliating! I was debating some kind of subtle reminder, but then he smiled and called "Hi!"

Not "Hi, Janet!" Just "Hi."

He'd probably forgotten my name was Janet, but I decided it was unrealistic to expect *too* much. And then, wonder of wonders, he began easing his bike over to the curb.

Oh, man! Were Karen and Star ever going to be impressed with me! Not only did I (supposedly) have this wonderful date for the dance, but I was on talking terms with a *guy like this!*

Colin half sat, half stood on the bike beside us, smiling that wide, sensitive smile. I couldn't believe how *old* he looked. Gee, he might even be *seventeen!* He was wearing nice dark green cords, a green-and-white checked shirt and Nikes. And a wristwatch. I *love* it when guys wear wristwatches. It's so *masculine*.

"Hi, Colin," I said. "This is my friend Karen Kepplewhite, and this is Star Sumner." I felt like adding, "And I'm Janet, Wilmer's sister, in case you've forgotten my name." I didn't, of course. That would have been too crass.

There is a test Karen and I have with guys. We call it the Star Test. Usually, when a boy sees Star for the first time, he is completely boggled. She doesn't have to say *one word,* dumb or otherwise, before he's panting at her feet. It's because of her naturally streaky blond hair and those big, violet eyes, etc., etc. And then there are people in this world who tell you that looks don't matter. What a lie!

The Star Test works this way. If the guy talks intelligently to any other girl who happens to be there instead of just goggling at Star, then we've decided he's VERY MATURE. Not too many guys pass, I have to admit. Karen says boys can't help it. Seeing Star for the first time is like seeing the Grand Canyon or Niagara Falls. I think Karen exaggerates a bit. At any rate, Colin O'Malley was definitely passing the Star Test. VERY, VERY mature, I decided. He was just saying "Hi" to her the way he said it to Karen and me.

I was thinking hard, trying to come up with a clever remark to impress him and to impress Karen and Star, too. Something to show them how *well* I knew him.

"I checked the library today for a D and D book," I said. "They *have* one, but it's out."

I had his full attention. There is one advantage to having a D and D freak for a brother, it gives you a definite insight into other D and D freaks. You *know* that to them Dungeons and Dragons is one of the most interesting things in the world.

"You looked for a book?" He was beaming at me. "You really *are* serious about learning. I'll tell you what. I have a copy of *A D and D Player's Guide*. It's the best. I'll lend it to you."

"Great!" I sneaked a quick glance at Karen and Star to make sure they were getting all of this. They were.

The light had changed, and Colin was about to push off.

"I'll bring the book when I come over tonight," he called.

"Sure," I said. "Anytime."

I could hardly stand it. Man, Karen and Star were *never* going to patronize me again! I bet they hadn't noticed that at the beginning he didn't know my name!

Karen was staring at me. "Janet Hamm!"

I tried to act cool. If ever there was a time for being nonchalant, this was it.

"*He's* the one, isn't he?" Karen asked. "Jeepers! I wouldn't keep HIM hidden."

Then she was hugging me and jumping up and down, right on the corner of Del Mar and California. Star was joining in, and people were looking at us and smiling. I guess everybody loves a bunch of happy kids. And there I was, gasping and spluttering, "The one? What do you mean, the one?"

Karen was strangling me. "And he's coming over tonight! Oh my gosh, Janet!"

I pried her arm from my neck. "He's a friend of Wilmer's. That's why he's coming over."

"Well, sure. You're so lucky to have an older brother. All Georgie brings home are worms and snails that he picks from under the rosebushes."

"Wait! Wait!" I said.

"Did you just meet him?" Star asked.

I nodded. Speechless. I'd never seen Star and Karen

look at me with such . . . such admiration!

Star clasped her hands and closed her eyes. "Francine Grady is going to have a total fit. I bet Colin's twice as nice as her stupid Marlboro man. What a *coup* for you!" She imitated Francine's snooty voice. "Coup means *prize,* in case you didn't know. All OLDER boys are coups."

Karen grinned and rolled her eyes.

"Before you go any further," I said. "Colin O'Malley did *not* invite me to the dance. I *swear.*"

"We know that. You invited him." Karen searched for words. "But he's so much . . . beyond us! How did you get up the nerve?"

"I didn't," I said. But they weren't listening.

"It's easy to tell he likes you." Star was nodding and beaming. "His eyes were sparkling when he was talking to you. Honest, Janet, it was as if you were the most interesting thing in the whole world."

"That's the D and D sparkle," I said. "Wilmer gets it too."

Karen gave me a sly glance. "You *did* tell us your date liked indoor games!"

We were passing 41 Flavors. I breathed in the cold chocolate and vanilla ice cream air and tried to think how to start my confession. It's hard to shoot sky-high in your friends' estimations, higher even than Star, and then have to come crashing down. Star for a Day, I thought. Star for five minutes.

"Let's tell Janet now about you-know-what!" Star said.

"Oh, let's!" Karen grabbed my arm. "I'm *so* glad we can tell you now. I hate having to keep secrets from you, Janet. Let's go into 41 Flavors, and sit on the patio, and get a double-nutty, double-chocolate cherry sundae and you can tell us all about Colin, and we'll tell you all about you-know-what."

"It wasn't that we didn't WANT to tell you," Star said.

Karen butted in. "It's just, you didn't have a date for the dance then. And I wasn't sure you'd even come." She paused. "I thought you probably *wouldn't* because of what Danny said. About the dog pen and all."

Karen knows me pretty well.

"But now it's okay," she added.

I decided to put off confessing just a little bit longer.

Chapter Seven

41 Flavors isn't as fancy as Trimble's Ice Cream Shop. But they have a nice patio with round tables and striped metal umbrellas, and a fountain that sometimes works and sometimes doesn't. Today it did. We sat next to it and ate out of our oversized paper cones. I'd bought a double-nutty, double-chocolate cherry sundae and so had Karen. Star got a mocha chocolate almond with coconut sprinkles. I tried not to think of it as symbolic that Karen and I were the same and Star was different.

"Are you going to tell me the secret now?" I asked. Was this AWFUL getting them to tell me under false pretenses? It probably was. But I wanted to know so BADLY.

Karen nodded. "What happened was this. Star's

Aunt Jeri Joe . . . you know, the one who lives on Altadena Drive?"

I nodded. "I haven't met her."

"Well, Aunt Jeri Joe sews real well, so Star phoned her, and told her about the dance, and she said she knew all about nifty fifties' dances because she'd been to a few of the real thing herself."

"She's older than my mom," Star explained. "She was a teenager then."

"And she told us she'd make us matching skirts for the dance. The kind they wore then, real wide, with POODLES on them!"

"Poodles?" I was boggled.

Karen's sundae was melting, so she ate a few spoonfuls fast. "First she thought she'd only be making skirts for Star and me, but I told her about YOU and she said, no problem, if you were going to the dance she'd make one for you, too. I didn't want to tell you though. Not till you were sure. Because not going to the dance would be awful enough, but to miss out on a poodle skirt, too!"

Karen shook her head at the awfulness of it. "The skirts will all be different colors, but the poodles will be black with darling fluffy balls for noses and cute fluffy tails."

"My skirt's going to be yellow," Star said. "Karen's having pink, and she told Aunt Jeri Joe yours should be blue."

"Blue's your best color," Karen said. "Is that okay,

Janet? Besides, I was thinking you could borrow my new blue T-shirt with the long sleeves. That would look super."

I swallowed. "It might be too tight. I mean, the T-shirt." I wonder why I sometimes feel like bawling when someone does something really nice for me. It doesn't make sense. Karen says her mother says you *never* really get over that, but that it's worse when you're thirteen. She says she used to bawl out loud all the time.

I looked at Karen and I wanted to go round the table and hug her. She'd have been surprised all right. Nice, true friend Karen, who'd included me even before she knew I was going. Who was lending me her newest, cutest T-shirt.

"Would you like another double-nutty double-chocolate cherry sundae, Karen?" I asked. "Or a mocha chocolate almond with coconut sprinkles? I've got two dollars left."

"Uh-uh." Karen licked her little plastic spoon. "I *couldn't*. But that one was so-ooo good!" She sat back. "Anyway, Aunt Jeri Joe says we should come up to her house on Saturday to get measured, you know, for the skirts."

"And she has little angora frills that you put on the top of your bobby socks," Star said. "And lacy collars. You pin the collar at the neck of your sweater, or your T-shirt. It's so great she kept all those things. She has them in a little lavender sachet so they're going to smell good too."

"And we'll be all the—" Karen stopped. "Janet! I've just thought of something horrible! Suppose Colin doesn't want to GO with us, and Mark and John. I mean, maybe he'll think we're too *babyish*. He's so OLD."

"Are you kidding?" I asked. "You're my best friends. If Colin goes with *me* he goes with *you,* too." I reminded myself of Kitten in "Father Knows Best." I was so loyal and so sincere! And suddenly I thought, what am I *saying?* Colin wasn't going with them or with me either. I'd been totally bowled over by the poodle skirts and the socks with the angora frills.

"It's . . . I . . ." I felt as if I were trapped in one of Georgie's mazes with no way out. I scratched back my chair and stood up fast. "I just remembered. I have to go to Penny's and water my carrot tree. It's . . . it's really nice of your aunt. Thanks, Star. Thanks, Karen." I began backing away, and I almost tripped over a pigeon that rose with a squawk from under my feet.

And then I was out of there and half running. I half ran all the way to Penny's. When I got to her yard, I threw myself into her swing so hard that the ropes quivered.

Karen and Star were going to HATE me when they found out. I reran the conversation in my head to see if I'd told any actual *lies* yet. From lies, there's no return. I'd have to stop Aunt Jeri Joe before she started on my skirt, before she bought the fabric. I felt like bawling again, for a sad reason this time.

What if Colin O'Malley found out he was supposed to be my date for the dance? What if Wilmer found out? He'd *kill* me!

Inside Penny's someone was making a terrible mess of "Für Elise." I could hear the patient murmur of Penny's voice and then "Für Elise" would start all over again, worse than ever. It was the saddest sound I'd ever heard in my life.

Oh brother! Was *I* in trouble! UNLESS . . . somewhere, in the back of my brain a cell began to quiver. I sat straighter in the swing. UNLESS . . . ? Could I possibly GET Colin to take me?

"Hi, Janet!"

It was the kid again. Rolf. He'd just come into Penny's yard with his music under his arm.

"Hi, Rolf." My mind was darting this way and that. I looked at Rolf but I scarcely saw him.

"Look!" He was pointing at my poor carrot tree, which I had totally forgotten. It looked as if someone had sneaked up on it and battered it to death with a heavy club.

"I don't think your tree's going to make it," Rolf said. "But I planted a carrot garden."

"You did?" I noticed then that the tree stood in the middle of a patch of smooth, brown earth.

I got down from the swing. It was amazing how much better I felt. Once you think of something to try, things just don't seem as hopeless anymore. Especially if the thought has just come to you, and you haven't had time to look at all its pitfalls. I walked across and peered down at the patch of smooth soil.

"You're supposed to put lines of string, and sow the seeds inside the lines," Rolf said. "But I didn't do that. I just brought a trowel and dug up the weeds and scattered the seeds like this." He waved his hand around to show me how he'd done it.

"You did all that since yesterday?"

"Sure. I don't start school till September so there's not much to do. I practice, and I go to the library, and I watch TV. That's about all. Besides, we only live a block away, and Penny says she likes carrots. She says she might even get a rabbit."

"A rabbit would be nice." I was feeling better all the time.

A girl came out on the porch. "Thank heaven! No more 'Für Elise'," I whispered.

"It was pretty bad," Rolf sounded real serious. "But she'll get better. Everyone's bad at the beginning."

I thought that was nice of him to say.

"Did you know Penny has ear plugs?" I whispered. "I saw them in her bathroom. She says they're because a bunch of dogs around here bark all night. Still. I always check to see if she has them in her ears when *I* have my lesson. I figure that would be a real bad sign."

"Rolf!" Penny called.

She waved to me, and I waved back.

"I'll water the garden right now," I told Rolf. "And if the rabbit and Penny don't want all the carrots, I'll make us a carrot cake." I'd never made a carrot cake. But right now everything seemed possible.

"Good," Rolf said.

All the time I was carrying cups of water from the porch, I thought about things I could do to persuade Colin to take me to the dance. Already I could tell that might not be as easy as baking a carrot cake.

I rushed home to begin my strategy.

Mom was sitting on the couch, reading the afternoon paper. She looked up and smiled, then patted the couch beside her. "Sit down a sec, Janet. I want to talk to you."

"You do?"

I didn't sit too close. Mom and I don't have heart-to-heart talks often and there was something about her expression that made me think that's exactly what this was going to be. I had a bad bottom-of-the-stomach feeling coming on.

Mom lifted a pillow, hugged it against her and stared into space.

"The house looks nice," I ventured. "You do too, Mom."

She smiled. "That's what I want to talk about. After

your dad . . . well, I guess I let everything go. Nothing seemed to matter anymore."

I remembered. She'd cried a lot, and her eyes were always bloodshot. They looked great today, clear and gray. She even had on some mascara.

She rested her chin on the pillow. "I realize now how dumb that was. I wasn't punishing your father. I was punishing myself, and you children. I'm still young. I'm not bad looking." She gazed straight at me. "I've neglected my responsibilities, and I want to say I'm sorry."

She realizes all this because of the guy, I thought. *He's* the one who told her she's not bad looking. That she's still young. Probably he told her she was gorgeous and sexy, and she's playing it down. I imagined him like a grown-up Danny DePuzo.

"I've started in the gym, trying to get myself in shape." Mom groaned an exaggerated groan. "And I've enrolled in P.C.C."

P.C.C. is our local community college.

"Sounds good." Just call me Miss *Janet Nonchalant Hamm*.

"I'm taking computer science. Jumping right into the new world, Janet."

"I'm glad, Mom." I was. But I was nervous, too. I could tell this guy was having quite an influence on her.

Mom reached out and touched my cheek. We're not a touching kind of family, and I was glad she didn't grab hold of my hand and keep it, because that would have been embarrassing.

"I'm going to need your help, Jan."

"How?"

"I have a long way to go. Be my friend. Talk to me." She grinned a lopsided kind of grin. "Tell me occasionally that the house looks nice. That I look nice. Give me a pat on the back if I bring home good grades."

"Sure." I wanted to say I could have used a bit of that myself these past years, but that didn't seem fair right now. And then *she* said it.

"I haven't given you much of that, Janet. Or Wilmer either. But today somebody reminded me that this is the first day of the rest of my life and to use it well. Corny, I know, and too easy. But true."

Somebody had told her. I knew who. I wished she'd level with me about him. It might make it less scary. Especially if I knew they weren't going to skip to Tahiti. Still, surely now she wouldn't want to leave the gym? And her computer class? I wondered what she'd say if I told her about the mess *I* was in, and how desperate I was to have Colin be my date for the dance.

I stood up. "Well, I've got homework."

"I'm going out for a while, dear. I'll bring back something for dinner."

"Okay." I was at the bottom of the stairs, and I glanced back through the living-room window. Colin and Wilmer were parking their bikes on our front porch.

My heart began to beat fast, and I told myself to cool it. To forget about Mom and her mystery man and concentrate now on Colin. I reminded myself not to be nervous. All I had to be was daring and self-confident and irresistible. It couldn't be all *that* hard.

Chapter Eight

Upstairs, I changed into my jeans and my white crop top. Actually, it's a white T-shirt with the bottom cut off. My jeans are probably the nicest, most grown-up thing I have, since they're fake designer. Karen and I each got a pair in a discount store, and believe me, Calvin Klein would *die* if he SAW the place!

I brushed my hair back and clipped on the pearl earrings Karen bought me last Christmas. She says pearls suit my skin tones. My new lip gloss whispers Kiss me! Kiss me! or so the commercials say. It's supposed to be totally irresistible. Wilmer says it whispers Slime-ee! Slime-ee! and is totally repulsive. But what does Wilmer know? I have matching pink Ever-Dewy nail polish, and I did my fingernails. I didn't bother with my toes because there was still some unchipped stuff on them.

In my clogs I'm at least a half inch taller. I stood sideways to the mirror and sucked in my stomach, thinking again how one of the unfairnesses of life is that I've got too much everywhere else and nothing on top. Oh well! I sprayed about three ounces of Heaven Scent at my pulse points, and I had to admit that right now I was pulsing a lot.

Okay. If my insides would stop heaving, I was ready.

I wafted down to the dining room and over to the table. "Hi, Wilmer! Hi, Colin!"

Wilmer wrinkled his nose and said, "Phew! Did you make that stuff yourself in the double boiler?"

If he'd said anything more, I swear I would have killed him. But I didn't need to worry. He and Colin were both poring over the game as if I'd never even appeared. I drummed my Ever-Dewy nails gently on Colin's side of the table.

"Did you remember to bring the book?" I asked, licking my lips for extra Kiss Me appeal.

"The book?" Colin gave me a blank look. He seemed to be still in elf land, or wherever. "Was I supposed to bring you a book?" He tapped the side of his head. "Sure. The *D and D Player's Guide*. I forgot. I'm sorry."

"It's all right. Maybe you can bring it tomorrow."

He frowned. "I don't think I'll be over tomorrow."

Oh, worse and worse. I stood, spreading my fingers

for full-on nail effect. But I might as well not have been there. It was so quiet in the dining room, I thought I could hear Wilmer and Colin concentrating. I could hear the living-room clock ticking. My heart was ticking just as loudly.

"Guess what, Colin? We're having an end-of-the-year dance at school."

Both heads stayed bent over the table. Outside, a mocking bird called yah-yah, yah-yah.

"My magician wants to cast a charm person," Wilmer said.

Criminy! What had that to do with our dance?

"Right." This was Colin, speaking in a clipped, businesslike way. "Make your dexterity roll."

Roll-smoll, I thought. "We don't *have* a D and D Club in school," I said, raising my voice. "And I just bet the kids would LOVE to get one started over summer. I mean, if they knew what it *was*. If someone could explain it to them."

Wilmer was rolling one of those funny-looking dice. "Four," he said. "My dexterity is thirteen. I made it by nine."

Baloney unlimited, I thought. Stupid game. I tried to keep desperation out of my voice.

"If they had a real dungeon master to . . . you know, EXCITE them. I could check it out with the leadership club if you like. But I know it would be okay. You could come to the dance, and I'd introduce you at the break. I'd tell about how you're a Dungeon Master and . . .

all the seventh graders will be there. It's on the eighth."
I was talking to the back of Colin's head as he consid-
ered that dumb vinyl sheet. No good. No good. I was
running down like a record after you pull the wall plug.
"Six thirty till ten," I mumbled.

Colin looked up and blinked. "What is?"

"The dance."

"Oh." He seemed to be having a hard time concentrating on me. "Okay," he said.

I stared at him. I swear to heaven I nearly died. Had
he said okay, or had I dreamed it?

"Did you say you'd come to the dance?" I asked.

"Sure."

Wilmer was staring at him too. "Are you crazy? This
is a seventh grade dance she's talking about, you nit-
wit."

"Wilmer!" Behind Colin's back, I made throat-
cutting signs at my brother.

"That's okay," Colin said again.

Slowly, carefully, I backed out of the room. He was
COMING. All my troubles were over! Oh, heaven! I
couldn't believe it! And so easy. Now I'd get to wear
the darling poodle skirt for *real*, and wouldn't Francine
Grady be GREEN with envy? And Danny DePuzo! "Is
that *you* in the dogpen, Danny DePuzo? I'd like to
introduce you to my date for the evening. His name is
Colin O'Malley, and he's in high school." No, I might
leave out that last part. Cool would be in and boasting
would be out. As Mr. Heflin, our principal, says about

broken windows and toilet-paper wads stuck on the ceiling, "The happening speaks for itself."

I raced back upstairs. Oh, Colin! How could I have thought that your nose was too long? Your nose is *perfect*. *You* are *perfect*.

I flung myself on my bed and dialed Mrs. Kepplewhite's number. How wonderful to be able to talk to Karen sincerely about the dance and Colin! I'd say, "He's the ONE all right. Isn't it incredible?"

"Kepplewhite residence," Georgie said.

"This is the Lord of the Dark Moon Planet," I growled and Georgie giggled and said, "It is not. It's Janet."

"Wow, you're smart!" I buffed my Ever-Dewy nails on my bedspread. "Is Karen there?"

"No. She's out. Hey, Janet? I've got a new puzzle book. You have to find things in the pictures. Gran and me can't find the witch's broom. Can you come over and help me?"

"I can't right now, Georgie. Is there a tree in the picture? Sometimes they hide the broom in the tree branches. Turn the picture upside down."

"Okay."

"Wait a sec," I yelled. "Don't go yet." I rolled over on my stomach and smiled. Heaven Scent wafted around me. It was nice that Georgie had forgiven me and was still my friend. "You know what, Georgie? I like you a whole bunch."

"Yeah, well, I don't like girls to like me."

"Do you know where Karen went?"

"Somewhere with Star."

"Oh." Somehow, knowing Star and Karen were doing something together didn't hurt as much anymore. They probably figured I'd be busy with Colin, and they were right. "Well, tell her to call me as soon as she gets home. Don't *forget*, Georgie."

"Okay."

"Wait, don't go yet. Ask your gran if she knows how to play Dungeons and Dragons. Tell her I might be helping to start a club."

He dropped the phone with a clang that almost took my ear off, and I heard him yell, "Gran?"

When he came back he said: "She says she'd like to learn. She says she's about finished learning to knit. Good-bye."

This clang was louder than the last one.

I lay down for a while, imagining me and Colin walking into the dance. He'd be looking a million times more mature than any other guy there, and my poodle skirt would be swaying as we crossed the floor, and everyone would be whispering "Check out the guy with Janet Hamm! Wow, what a superfox!"

Oh, criminy, I felt so good.

I lay for a while more and then I called the library and asked if they had any D and D books. The librarian said yes, and I told her to save them for me and I'd be right over.

Colin and Wilmer didn't even look up as I came

through the dining room. Man, this Dungeons and Dragons was INTENSE. I drifted partway to the table and raised my voice.

"I'm off to the library. They've got some D and D books on hold for me. I think the sooner I start learning, the *better*. I'll be able to introduce you with . . . with more pizzazz, Colin. And then, when you start your club, I'll know a lot and if you like, I can be your assistant."

"Good idea," Colin muttered. "Look out for Roach the Thief," he said loudly, which I guess had some connection to the game and was addressed to Wilmer and not to me.

The librarian had *Deities and Demigods, Fiend Folio* and *The Dungeon Master's Guide*. I took them all.

"I *know* a Dungeon Master," I told her as she was checking out the books.

"That's nice," she said and sneezed.

"He's over at my house right now."

She didn't look as boggled as I'd expected.

"He's my *date* for the school dance," I said.

She gave me back my card and sneezed again. I guess librarians aren't that easy to boggle.

"I seem to be allergic to something rather suddenly," she said. "Are you wearing perfume?"

"Just a little." I retreated.

Someone said, "Hi, Janet!"

It was Rolf. He was sitting at one of the polished wood tables by the magazine racks.

I went across, plunked my books down and sat opposite him.

Rolf picked up *Fiend Folio.*

"Dungeons and Dragons," I said. "It's a terrific game."

"I've never played it."

Probably too young. Just because Rolf was a musical genius didn't mean he was smart at everything. "It's sort of a MATURE game." I looked to see what he was reading. "*Gourmet Cooking?* No kidding?"

"Did you know you can make carrot jelly?" Rolf asked. "And carrot soufflé. And even carrot Christmas tree ornaments. There's no end to what you can make out of carrots."

"My brother Wilmer drinks carrot juice," I said. "Wilmer drinks *everything.* If we have a good crop, we'll give him some to juice."

I leaned across the table. There are some things that are too exciting to keep to yourself. "You know what?" I asked. "I just got a date for the school dance. I think he's sixteen."

Rolf was definitely boggled.

I smiled happily.

"Gee, Janet," he said. "There must be somebody younger than *that* who'd want to take you."

"You don't GET it," I said. "Older is better. There's

this girl, Francine Grady. . . ." I stopped. "It's too hard to explain. But believe me, getting a sixteen-year-old is a real coup." I gathered up my books.

"Janet?"

"Yes?"

"I'm not that crazy about carrot anything, if you want to know the truth. I really planted the garden for you."

"I know. That was real nice."

"Well," Rolf took off his glasses and polished them on his shirt. "I don't know anybody, you see. And I wanted to be your friend."

"Sure," I said. "I'll be your friend. And once your school starts after summer, you'll have scads of friends. See you, Rolfie!"

I was a little tense as I headed for the swinging barrier that lets you out of the library. It dings if you're stealing a book. Danny DePuzo has a buzzer that makes the same sound, and he sometimes buzzes when a girl's going through. It makes a person all the time NERVOUS! But today was okay. Which meant Danny wasn't around.

I had to do a balancing act on the way home, since I had all those books and no book bag. When I got there, the first thing I noticed was that Colin's ten-speed was not parked next to Wilmer's on the porch. He hadn't gone, had he? I still had to make final arrangements about the dance. He'd probably call, though. Or I'd call him. Wilmer would know his number.

I flung open the door.

Wilmer was tidying up the table, putting the little dice into a drawstring bag.

"What happened?" I asked. "Where's Colin?"

"The Paladin rescued the Enchanted Princess," Wilmer said. "The game's over. It didn't take as long as we'd thought."

"Did Colin say anything? I mean, about me? About the dance?"

Wilmer tossed the dice bag from one hand to the other. "Well, yeah . . ." His eyes darted in my direction and away.

Something inside me began to slump. I had definite feelings of dread. "Oh, Wilmer, don't tell me," I begged.

"I don't want to. But I think I'd better." Wilmer heaved the bag on top of the vinyl sheet. In the quiet I could hear his knuckles begin to go crack, crack, crack.

Chapter Nine

Wilmer pulled one of the dining-room chairs around to face me. It was the place where Colin had sat. I had this horrible, sure feeling that Wilmer was going to tell me something bad about HIM.

"The thing is," Wilmer said slowly. "Colin doesn't *listen* carefully when he's involved with D and D."

I had to lick my Kiss Me lips before I could speak. "You mean, he didn't listen to me asking him to the dance? You mean, I have to ask him all over again?"

Wilmer sat straight. "No. Don't do that, Janet. Colin heard you. Sort of. He heard the D and D part."

"But he said he'd *go*."

"He said he'd go tell them about starting a D and D Club. He'd make an announcement. He said you could introduce him."

"Uh-uh. Uh-uh." I was shaking my head so hard that one of my pearl earrings flew across the floor. Wilmer went after it and brought it back.

"You were THERE, Wilmer. You know what I said."

"He didn't know. I thought he was nuts, remember? Tenth grade guys do not go to dances with silly little seventh graders."

I let the insult pass, which shows the kind of state I was in.

Wilmer held out the pearl earring. It lay like a teardrop on his hand. I took it, rolled it between my fingers and went forlornly to the living-room couch. I sat on the arm.

"The fact is"—Wilmer sat too, properly on the couch—"Colin *has* started a couple of D and D clubs. One in the Hill Avenue Library. One in the Y. One in the Boys' Club. He didn't think it was strange when you asked him to start one in Roosevelt. I didn't tell him what you were *really* asking, because he had no idea, and I figured you wouldn't want me to clue him in."

He was right. That would have been too embarrassing.

"I told him he should forget about starting the club. That I thought it would be a bad idea. You'd have had a hard time handling that, too."

"Yeah. But, Wilmer! Maybe I should try for the *dance* part again? If he didn't get what I meant last time—"

"No way, toots. Anyway, Colin has a girl friend. Her name's Donna, and she's a big wheel in the drama club in school."

"A girl friend? I bet she looks like a dragon and smells like a dungeon. That's the only kind of a dumb girl THAT dumb boy would be interested in."

Wilmer grinned, reached up and tweaked my hair. "He's way too old for you, anyway."

"No, he isn't. And besides, I've gone and told a lot of people."

"Already? That was fast!"

"I told the librarian. And Rolf. And I almost told Karen, only she wasn't there."

"So? Just say you made a mistake."

"But Wilmer! You don't understand. Now I'm back where I started. I STILL don't have a date for the dance. I *thought* I had, for—for a glorious HOUR. Now I'm back to being a DOG."

Oops! A real tear had dropped on the back of my hand. I couldn't believe it. This past week I'd felt like crying a whole bunch of times. It had been like rain coming, and now the storm had hit. Even holding my nose and swallowing fast weren't going to stop it.

I thought about the poodle skirt, and I cried harder. I slid off the arm of the couch onto the cushions beside Wilmer and sobbed.

Wilmer was boggled all right.

He put his arm around my shoulder and said, "It's okay, Janet." and "Don't cry" and stuff like that. Wilmer doesn't put his arm around my shoulder that often. He was probably dying to crack his knuckles, but his hands were too far apart.

"Everything's awful," I wailed.

"*I'll* take you, if you like."

"Oh, Wilmer!" That made me cry even harder. "I didn't think you even *liked* me."

"Of course, I like you. You're my sister."

I didn't say he'd never shown any signs of liking me *before*. Maybe it takes a tragedy like this to bring families together.

"I really appreciate you asking me, Wilmer. But I *can't* go with my BROTHER. Going with a brother would be worse than not going at all. No offense."

Wilmer was patting my back and looking scared. "Did Mom say where she was off to?"

"Probably to Tahiti," I said. "With him. By themselves. Nobody wants to take ME anywhere."

Wilmer was patting me so hard it hurt. "She's not going to Tahiti, Janet. She's not going anywhere. Look, she doesn't even *have* a boyfriend. That was all pretend. Don't cry anymore. Mom's not going to leave us."

He sat up and reached across me for the phone. "I found this number in her little black book. It was all ringed around in hearts."

"I know."

"So last night I dialed it, just to see who was on the other end.

"Wilmer! You didn't! I almost did too." Now I had hiccups. I put my hand over my mouth. "Excuse me."

Wilmer dialed and held the phone out to me. "Listen!"

I pulled away.

"Take it," he said. "It's okay. Honest."

I took the phone, and Wilmer got up and disappeared into the kitchen. He came back with the roll of paper towels.

"I wasn't crying *that* much," I said. "And what am I supposed to talk about when this guy . . . ?" I stopped.

"Hi," the voice on the phone said. The man's voice. "This is Adonis, your fantasy lover."

"What?" I signaled for Wilmer to get over here, but he shook his head. "Keep listening," he said.

"Tonight I thought we'd go to that little Moroccan restaurant you liked so much. The one beside the river. Remember how we ate by candlelight and outside the moon rose silver in the sky?"

"Hic," I said. "Excuse me. I think I got the wrong number."

Adonis went right on talking. He had a voice like black velvet. "I took your hands in mine and told you how much I loved you, and the waiter came and heard us, and he smiled and moved away." Adonis laughed a low romantic laugh. "And later we danced on the patio, under the stars, and I bought a gardenia for your hair?"

I put my hand over the mouthpiece. "Who *is* this bozo and what's he talking about?" I was so astonished

I'd almost forgotten Colin and the *terrible misunderstanding*.

Wilmer wiggled his eyebrows. "You ain't heard nothin' yet!" He pushed on the phone buttons to disconnect and dialed again. "Which one was that? What was he telling her?"

"About dancing by the river."

"I don't think I've heard that one. Here's another. Try this."

"Hi," the same dark velvet voice said. "This is Adonis, your fantasy lover. Last night I dreamed we were walking in the forest again. The sun made shadows on the pine needles at our feet. We didn't talk. Have you noticed how many good silences we have, my love? When we got to the clearing, I pulled you close. Your lips were cold, and your hair smelled of sunlight. When I kissed you . . ."

I held the phone away. "This is embarrassing. He's kissing her in the clearing, and her hair smells of sunlight."

"That's a good one," Wilmer said. "But the one about running along the sands in Tahiti is the best of all."

He took the phone from me and set it back on the hook.

"They're *records?*" I asked.

"Yeah. The guy must be making a fortune. It's probably at least fifty cents a time. But I guess if you're lonely, it's worth it."

"That's sad," I said. I thought about how I'd blamed Mom a lot for not knowing how *I* felt. Well, what about her?

"I guess he was good for Mom, though," Wilmer said, "He gave her a boost when she needed it."

I held out my hand for the paper towels. "Too bad he wasn't the real thing."

"Oh, I don't know. What you *imagine* you'd like to have probably isn't what you want at all. I mean, wouldn't it be gross to have a guy talking to you that way IN PERSON? He'd be a joke! And imagine having a stepfather named Adonis?"

Wilmer grinned, and I semigrinned back. I blew my nose a second time and felt better.

"Here's something else." Wilmer picked up Mom's phone book and opened it. "Adonis's number was right here. Now the page is gone."

I looked at the raggedy edge of paper. "Maybe she put it in her underwear drawer?"

"Uh-uh. It was crumpled up in the trash when I emptied the garbage this morning."

I hiccuped. "You're such a snoop, Wilmer."

Wilmer threw himself back in the couch beside me. "I'm good, all right. See those other two numbers? She probably wrote those down when she got them from information. One's the gym. One's P.C.C. class schedules. See? She exchanged the 'not real' for the real."

He closed the book. "You know what I bet? That she finds somebody nice. Somebody who wants to be her friend. I mean, she didn't even KNOW this guy!" Wilmer was whistling and staring off into space. "Could be he was way too old for her. Could be they have nothing in common."

"Oh, like subtle, Wilmer," I said sarcastically. "You're not by any chance digging at me and Colin, are you?"

"Would I do that?" Wilmer asked.

But I was thinking all the same. I was thinking about what he'd said.

Chapter Ten

"Somebody nice. Somebody who wants to be her friend." Wilmer could have been talking about Rolf. Not for Mom, of course, but for me.

I gathered up the books and cycled back to the library. No use reading these now. And anyway, if I went right away, Rolf might still be there.

The same librarian was behind the desk. "Returning these already?" she asked.

I nodded.

"My, you *are* a quick study," she said and sneezed. To think that my Heaven Scent was still working after all I'd been through! I might write them a letter of congratulations.

When I squinted sideways, I could see that Rolf was

still at the table, and my heart began going bumpity-bump. I sauntered over, very nonchalant.

He seemed to have given up on carrot reading and was now surrounded by *Car* magazine and the *Musician*.

"Hi," I said. "I'm back."

"Oh, hi, Janet."

I picked up a copy of the *Musician* and began turning pages. "When's your recital?"

"In July. Penny's going to invite all her students, I guess. I guess that means you, too. But it's okay if you don't want to go."

"I'd like to. Honest."

"You would?" Rolf's face was kind of pink.

"As long as you don't play 'Für Elise.'"

"No way." We grinned at each other, and I took a deep breath. Oh, what if I ended up asking *three* boys . . . *three,* and they *all* said no. What if Rolf said, "Not even if you stood me on my head! Not even if you were Princess Leia. Not if I were Paladin, and you were the Enchanted Princess." I gripped the edge of the table. It was now or never, before I totally lost my courage. "Would you like to go to the seventh grade dance with me, Rolf?"

He didn't answer, and my stomach gave a great gurgle. I pretended enormous interest in *Car* magazine. An ad inside said: "Some traditions never change . . . new electronically fuel-injected engine . . . contemporary, beautifully crafted instrument panel." Wasn't three supposed to be the magic number? Three coins in the fountain? Three wishes?

"What about the older guy?" Rolf asked.

I tossed my head. "That was a total lack of communication. He's really more into clubs than school dances."

"You mean discos? Jazz clubs, places like that?"

"It's too hard to explain." I was still standing, and my knees felt weak. I slid into the seat on the other side of the table. "I was thinking, Rolf. Going to the Roosevelt dance would be a way for you to meet other kids. You know, you said you didn't know any. And besides . . ."

"I'd like to go," Rolf said.

"You would? No kidding?" I could feel myself beaming. My face was probably red to explosion point. "Criminy Christmas! For a second there I thought you were going to say *no* and that would have been *awful*." I stopped. "You understand, I'm asking you to be my DATE, not to interest kids in Dungeons and Dragons or . . ."

"I don't even KNOW Dungeons and Dragons. Besides, I just want to go with you."

I straightened the magazines on the table. This was going to be hard to say too. "I know it's not GREAT to be someone's second choice. But honest, I do like you, Rolf. I just never thought of you for the dance."

"That's okay."

I leaned forward. "I *may* have trouble getting permission from Miss Wilson at the office, because actually this is supposed to be only for Roosevelt kids. But Francine Grady got permission for the Marlboro man, and I don't see the difference. Actually, younger SHOULD be better. What grade will you be in in September anyway?"

"Eighth. At Roosevelt. Same as you. I don't think you'll have any trouble, because they know in the office that I'll be registering."

Rolf smiled. I'd never noticed before what a truly adorable smile he has. "I know I don't look that old, but I'll probably spring up over the summer. That's what my dad says happened to him. It's a biological fact that boys grow more over the summer between seventh and eighth grade than at any other time in their lives."

"It is? You will?" I was boggled. "And you're really *thirteen*? I mean, it would be OK even if you weren't and even if you don't grow any more. But this way is terrific. Actually, I *like* boys who aren't too big," I added, just in case he had his biological facts wrong. "Do you think your dad might be transferred someplace else real soon?" I asked, remembering that in this life you can't take anything for granted.

"Uh-uh. We just GOT here," Rolf said.

I couldn't seem to stop smiling.

Rolf piled up the magazines. "I'll walk you home, if you like."

"I'm on my bike."

"I'll push it."

"Okay." I really like decisive boys.

"What time is it, anyway?" Rolf pushed back his sleeve and studied his watch. It had a black face and a black strap. I think it's the kind you can wear underwater, and it looked really mature on his wrist. In fact, his wrists looked really mature too, and strong. Not grossly thin and bony. I think if I'd noticed his wrists before, I'd have known he was thirteen.

As we strolled together across the library, I realized Rolf wasn't *that* small. If he grew two inches over the summer, he'd only be about two inches shorter than I am. As long as I didn't grow too.

"Miss Hamm?" The sneezy librarian was calling to me from behind the desk.

"Yes?" I ran across, light as a breeze.

"One of the clerks was telling me that there's a Dungeons and Dragons Club in the Hill Avenue Branch Library. A student who's very good is instructing them on how to play. Since you've read all the books and seem to be so interested, I thought I'd just let you know."

"Thanks. But I'm a little off D and D right now." I leaned forward for her to put her head closer to mine. I could see that the poor lady was holding her breath in case my Heaven Scent reached her nose again, so I spoke quickly.

"I just got a date for the school dance. He's waiting for me by the door."

She looked over my shoulder, sort of squinting under her glasses. "He's very nice," she said. "Congratulations."

"Thanks." I hoped I didn't look sappy, grinning all the time like this.

"Ready?" Rolf asked.

I nodded.

As we walked home, I thought about Karen and Star. How surprised they'd be! How surprised that Rolf wasn't Colin. Uh-oh. I hoped they weren't *disappointed!* I'd have to prepare them.

I realized my main problem was over. But I still had a couple of little ones lurking around the edges and quite a bit of explaining to do.

Chapter Eleven

I told Karen and Star about Rolf on the way home from school the next day. I guess I was still smiling because Karen said, "Well, jeepers, Janet. He must be TERRIFIC if you like him better than Colin!"

"I do," I said. "Rolf and I have MUCH more in common. And besides, Colin *is* too old. I mean, sixteen is getting UP there, and it might have been awkward."

We were quiet for a minute, thinking of all the awkward ways it might have been. Actually, some of that awkward stuff might have been totally exciting!

I was pleased with the way I'd gotten out of the Colin affair. And I still hadn't lied. Not about anything. But still. Not being really honest with Karen and Star was taking some of the fun out of having a REAL date for the dance.

"Imagine, Jan!" Karen said. "You had a *choice!* Not too many girls have a *choice!*" She sounded so admiring, almost in AWE of me, that it was tempting to let it go. But that didn't seem fair either.

"How about going to 41 Flavors to celebrate," I said. "My treat. And besides, I have a bunch of things to tell you."

We sat next to the fountain, which by some miracle was splashing again today. And I told them all. All about how I'd felt so left out in the beginning that I'd been describing *Georgie.*

They were boggled.

"Creepy little Georgie Kepplewhite?" Karen gasped "Horrors!"

"It's okay. He turned me down." And then I told them about Colin and the big misunderstanding and how nice Wilmer had been, offering to take me himself.

Karen shuddered. "*Your* brother or *my* brother! Criminy! Poor Janet!"

I didn't like that Poor Janet bit so I moved on quickly to Rolf. And pretty soon I was beaming again.

"I think it's very romantic, meeting by a carrot tree," Karen said.

Star clasped her hands together. "And making a garden for you, Janet. That's *so* nice."

"Rolf's *really* nice. But he's kind of small," I said. Best to tell them and get it over. "He'll probably grow over the summer, though."

Star and Karen nodded.

"He's great at piano, too," I added. "You'll see."

But I couldn't help having a little, sneaking worry still. Had I prepared them enough for Rolf? All this time I'd been giving my "secret date" such a buildup. That's the trouble with big buildups. Sometimes they lead to big letdowns.

The poodle skirts were ready and they were fabulous, soft and wide and so flattering!

Karen and Star and I had a dress rehearsal at Karen's after school on the day before the dance. Her mom and dad were home from Europe, and they'd brought darling silver chains with initials for the three of us. A *K*, an *S*, and a *J*. Two weeks ago I would have been jealous that Star got a chain too. It put her on the same friendship level with Karen and me. Now I wasn't jealous. Well, maybe a little, but not *intensely*. I mean, we all had chains, we all had poodle skirts, and we all had dates for the dance. In a way we were on the same level. It mightn't always be this way, but for now it was nice.

Aunt Jeri had come through with the angora ankle cuffs and the lace collar, too. I pinned mine on Karen's blue T-shirt. The shirt *was* a little tight. I didn't like to say it, and I guess Karen and Star didn't want to say it either. I decided to try my white sweater with the skirt instead as soon as I got home.

We practiced putting our hair in ponytails and trying different lip glosses to be sure they'd look good under the lights. My Kiss Me was the best, but you had to use a lot. We passed it around.

When we'd finished with the makeup, we inspected each other. Star was *gorgeous,* naturally. Karen looked really pretty, and wonder of wonders, I looked okay too. I think I have the answer to that question about whether you get prettier when you have a boyfriend. The answer is yes. Of course, Rolf isn't my *boyfriend* exactly. But he *is* my date for the dance.

"I wish we were going now," Karen said suddenly. "Just the three of us together."

"Without boys? Now that I *have* one?" I was aghast.

Karen bit her lip. "Well, I'd want to *see* the boys when we got there. It's just, this is scary, having them come and pick you up. What if Mark doesn't even *get* here? He's so shy."

"You know what?" I said. "You should wait for him on the porch. It would be awful if he were too shy to ring the doorbell."

"It's probably worse for THEM," Star said. "They have to come in and let the mothers and fathers look them over."

"And the LITTLE BROTHERS!" Karen rolled her eyes. "I'm going to ask Mom to lock Georgie *up* tomorrow night. Can you imagine?"

Star leaned forward to inspect her teeth in the mirror. Even with a snarling expression like that, Star's pretty. "Did you hear that Danny DePuzo's going to bring not one girl but a 'whole bunch' to the party?"

Karen giggled. "It must be a bunch of bananas."

Oh, it was so NICE to be able to laugh and to feel SECURE. "Only a banana would *go* with Danny De-Puzo," I said, and then I felt a little guilty because I remembered that I'd been wishing and wishing Danny would ask ME. Of course, at that point I'd been truly desperate.

"A bunch of 'really great babes.'" Karen imitated Danny perfectly. "'Why settle for ONE when I can handle a dozen?'"

"He must be taking the whole girls' soccer team," Star said, and we giggled.

We put some records on and danced. Star knows how to E. T. which is a spacey kind of dance, like something from another planet.

"Let's just hope it's not *all* fifties' stuff tomorrow night," Karen said.

"Let's hope!"

The words *tomorrow night* sobered us up. Tomorrow night they'd meet Rolf. So what if they didn't think he was that terrific? *I* did. But still.

We sighed three long sighs and then, without anybody arranging it, we grasped hands.

I have to admit, it is comforting to have *two* good true friends with whom to share the scary things of life. And this dance with dates was definitely one of the scariest.

Chapter Twelve

I was ready at five o'clock the next night, though Rolf wasn't supposed to pick me up till six fifteen.

Getting ready EARLY is *not* a good idea. I had to keep standing in case I creased my skirt, and my socks kept slipping down, which made me nervous about the rest of the night. I put an elastic band under each angora cuff and comforted myself that I did look pretty good. Not skinny, or blond, which would have been a miracle. But pretty good.

The most astonishing thing had happened the night before. Mom had come in my room.

"I bought you something for the occasion," she said, sort of shyly.

The "something" was in an I. MAGNIN box, so I knew it had to be good. It was. It was an angora sweater of pale, pale blue, so soft and fuzzy you wanted to hold it in your lap and stroke it.

"Oh, Mom, thank you!" I whispered and hugged her. The hug wasn't planned, but it worked out great.

"Angora sweaters were big in the fifties," Mom said. "I had a pale yellow one myself." I wondered if she'd worn it for Dad, but if she had and if she was thinking of him now, she didn't look sad a bit. In fact, she hadn't had that sad, hopeless look in a long time.

I hoped Adonis was making a pile of money on his tapes. I knew, of course, that he didn't deserve *all* the credit. But he hadn't hurt.

"I guess you didn't think I looked too great in Karen's T-shirt," I said. "I felt like I was wearing a *girdle* on *top*."

Mom had smiled. "This is prettier."

So here I was, waiting for Rolf in my blue fuzzy sweater with the pinned-on lace collar, the soft poodle skirt, and the cuffed bobby socks, complete with hidden bands.

"You're looking Killer, toots," Wilmer said, tweaking my ponytail.

"Looking Killer" is Wilmer's ULTIMATE compliment.

Just then the doorbell rang and it was Rolf. His white T-shirt sleeves were rolled up on to his shoulders and his baggy blue jeans were turned up to show white socks and black shoes. He'd sleeked down his nice hair and combed it back in a ducktail. I was glad he'd told me he was thirteen because, truthfully, he looked about ten.

"You are perfect," Mom told him. "Just like a young James Dean."

"Thanks." Rolf shuffled around a bit. He pointed to one of his rolled-back sleeves. "You're supposed to keep a pack of cigarettes in here. Of course, I don't smoke."

Mom had already talked to Rolf's mom on the phone and now she came out to speak to his dad, who was driving us over and who was standing by the car. I liked him right away when he said, "You look very nice, Janet. I wouldn't mind taking you to the dance myself."

He opened the door for me, and straight off I noticed how TALL he was. Could that *possibly* have all happened in the summer between seventh and eighth grade? Anyway, it was a good omen.

Rolf and I sat in the backseat with a wide space between us.

"Did you tell Janet what Miss Wilson asked you to do, Rolf?" his dad asked as we pulled up in front of the auditorium.

"No." Rolf spoke quickly and then said, "Don't forget, Dad. We'll be out here on the steps at ten o'clock."

I hoped Miss Wilson hadn't asked him for PROOF that he was going to Roosevelt, or something equally hideous. Whatever, Rolf didn't seem to want me to know.

The decorating committee had done a great job.

There were streamers and balloons everywhere, and even a revolving light with mirrors on it that dangled from the ceiling.

Swinging old-fashioned music filled the room, and I saw Star and John dancing over by the platform. I spotted Karen and Mark, too. What a relief! Mark had come as planned. It would have been too awful if he'd chickened out at the last minute!

Karen waved, and Rolf and I began pushing through the dancers. My poodle skirt swung against my legs. My ponytail bounced. I'd gone easy on the Heaven Scent in case I gave Rolf a sneezing fit, but I'd sprayed on enough to be subtle and alluring. I felt Rolf was definitely appreciating it.

One of my socks had slipped already, in spite of the rubber band, but I didn't think it was noticeable. And best of all, I was walking beside my *date!* But already I was wondering what Karen and Star would think of him, since they were seeing Rolf for the first time.

Now I had to make the introductions, and I was definitely nervous. It's all very well to tell yourself it doesn't matter *what* your friends think. But it does matter, secretly and inside.

"Rolf . . . this is Karen and Mark and Star and John," I said. "Everybody, this is Rolf." I held my breath.

Karen made a soundless "He's *darling!*" behind his back, and I nodded and beamed. I should have known Karen had good taste. Star was nodding and smiling, too. It was going to be all right.

Mark and John were wearing their jeans turned up on the bottoms, same as Rolf. They even had their T-shirt sleeves rolled back. I guess boys all dressed the same in the fifties, which must have been pretty boring.

Karen and Star went bananas over my blue angora sweater, and I said they could both borrow it for special occasions. And then we stopped to listen, because someone was speaking very loudly from the platform.

I looked up, and I couldn't believe what I was seeing. Karen began to giggle.

"Who *is* that?" Rolf asked.

"Danny DePuzo," I said, sounding as boggled as I felt.

"Well, gals and goons," Danny said in that smart-alecky way of his. "This is your very own DJ for the evening, Danny the Puzo himself, with music for your dancing pleasure. Let's swing and sway now to the happy sounds of Tommy Dorsey and his Big Band."

Actually, to say that I was boggled was putting it mildly. There was Danny the Puzo wearing dark pants and one of those nutty looking T-shirts that's printed to look like a tuxedo. It had painted-on lapels, a painted white ruffled shirt and even a carnation in the painted buttonhole. And he'd painted a mustache on himself!

I was speechless, which isn't something that happens to me too often. "He's the DISC JOCKEY? But what about the 'bunch of babes' he was bringing?"

"We *asked* him." Karen turned so I could straighten

her collar at the back. "He said he brought the best babes around. Doris Day. Peggy Lee. Kay Starr."

"Who are *they?*" I wasn't getting it.

"Real famous singers of the fifties," John said. "Danny brought the records."

Francine Grady had come up beside us. She introduced us to Chance, and I introduced her to Rolf. I didn't miss her superior little smile—she obviously thought Chance was WAY better!

Dumb Francine didn't know much! I had to admit that Chance *did* look like the Marlboro man. But I also noticed that he was chewing gum very loudly and looking bored to death. He was probably wishing already that he'd never come to a silly little seventh grade dance. And where had I heard *that* before?

"Isn't it hilarious about Danny?" Francine asked, and oh, were her eyes slitty! "It was just the way I thought. He couldn't get anyone to go with him so he had to make it up about all those 'cute chicks.'"

I wanted to join in with her, because I can't stand Danny myself. But somehow I felt very gracious tonight. And I was suddenly remembering the pleading way Danny had asked STAR to go with him on that very first day. Maybe Danny had known right from the start that he'd have trouble getting a date for the dance. I could sympathize with *that* all right.

"Nobody likes to be put down, Francine," I said. "So sometimes people make stuff up, so they can feel better. So other people can't *rub it in!*"

"Are you saying *I* rub it in?" Francine's eyes were slittier than ever. She pulled Chance's arm, but Chance was chewing his gum and staring over her head.

"Danny makes a really great disc jockey," nice Star said.

Francine tossed her hair. Ponytails don't toss very well. And frizzy red hair doesn't look that good in a ponytail either.

"Want to dance, Janet?" Rolf asked.

One of Danny's fifties' 'babes' was singing something about "IT'S MAGIC." It really was.

"Janet's date's awfully *small!*" I heard Francine whisper to Karen as Rolf and I passed. She's so rude. I just hope *Rolf* didn't hear.

"Expensive things come in small packages," Karen said coldly. Nice Karen!

And then Rolf and I were dancing to the slow, dreamy music. He was a really good dancer. It didn't matter a bit that he was shorter than I am. In fact, that just made him bouncier. I cast a couple of glances toward where the dog pen should have been, but I didn't see it. I think Danny just made that up to be mean. All I saw were girls and guys standing around, the way they'd be at any dance.

"Okay, you groovers!" Danny said. "Let's jive! Let's boogie! Here's an oldie but a goodie from the Count himself, the one, the only Count Basie."

We were all really into the fast music then, and it was great. Rolf kept swinging me out, pulling me back. He *does* have strong arms. And then someone tapped me on the shoulder, and I turned and saw Miss Wilson from the office.

She smiled. "Excuse me, kids."

For a minute I thought she wanted to dance with Rolf. Or with me.

"Uh-oh," Rolf said nervously, and I immediately got nervous too. Maybe he shouldn't BE here. Maybe he'd pretended things too. Maybe she'd found out he was only *eleven!*

"You're on!" Miss Wilson said. "I hope you're up for it, Rolf. Our DJ, Mr. Danny DePuzo, is just about to introduce you."

"Oh crumbs!" Rolf rubbed his hands together. "I *never* feel good before I start."

And I was saying, "Start what? What, Rolf? What?"

"You mean he hasn't told you?" Miss Wilson was smiling again. "I bent the rules a little and let Rolf come to the dance, even though he's not *quite* a Roosevelt student yet. Of course, I *had* made an exception for Francine to bring her cousin. But that was on special request from Francine's parents."

"The Marlboro man's her *cousin?*"

Miss Wilson was rattling on. "So, because I was so nice to Rolf he agreed to . . ."

She was interrupted by a great crashing of drums from the platform.

"Gals and geezers," Danny said. "Your attention!" He was standing by a set of drums that I guess had been up there all the time covered with a sheet. "Boys and babes, we have a special treat for you. Mr. Rolf Callison, who is here tonight as the date of Miss Janet Hamm, will play the drums for us."

"It was just a small case of blackmail," Miss Wilson whispered to me.

I scarcely heard her. "The date of Miss Janet Hamm"! For that I could forgive Danny anything.

But was Rolf really going to . . . ? I still couldn't take it in.

Then Miss Wilson was escorting Rolf and me through the crowd to the side steps of the platform. She and I stood while Rolf went up and sat behind the set of drums.

Criminy! He looked so pale. I felt pale myself.

"Are you sure he can play those?" I whispered to Miss Wilson. "Wouldn't it have been better to get a PIANO?"

"He can play them," Miss Wilson said. "And very well. This is his own drum set."

Everyone was quiet now, clustered around the platform. Rolf picked up the drumsticks and balanced them in his hands. For a minute I thought he'd started, and then I realized that was my *heart* going boom, boom, boompity, boom. The blue angora sweater was HOT. I pulled it away from me at the waist to get some air.

And then Rolf brought the sticks down on the drums, moving them slowly at first, then picking up the beat and going faster and faster. He hit the tom-toms. He hit the high hat. He added a little cymbals, and after that he seemed to go crazy.

Everybody was clapping now, and Rolf's hair had come out of its ducktail and was flying across his face. *So* adorable.

"Wow! Is he ever good!"

"Janet! He's terrific. He should be on 'Video One'."

"Or 'Dancin' California.'"

My hands were clenched, and I made them relax. How fabulous!

The drumsticks were moving so fast now that they were blurred. Feet stomped the floor. There was no way you could *stop* stomping and tapping.

When Rolf finished with a great crashing bang, the kids began yelling "More! More!"

Danny DePuzo came strutting over to Rolf, smiling his cat smile under the fake mustache, holding up his hand for quiet. "If you're all good, I may be able to get Rolf to do it one more time."

"Yeah! Yeah! One more time!"

Rolf was looking down at me and SMILING.

Behind me someone whispered, "He's with Janet Hamm. He's her date."

I could have died of happiness.

Afterwards I loaned Rolf a tissue to wipe his face, and then I put it carefully in my pocket for a souvenir.

"He's so NICE, Janet," Star said when she and Karen

and I were in the girls' room, freshening up our Kiss Me lips.

"I know." I took off my shoe and pulled up my sock.

"And to think," Karen added. "You could have been here with Georgie Kepplewhite. And he could have been playing his flute!"

Star got this dreamy look on her face. "I *really* liked a boy in fifth grade. He was the smallest boy in the class, and he was so cute. All the girls liked him. He could make great animal noises, you know, dogs growling and cats meowing? One day, Mrs. Goldblatt, she was our teacher, well, she was sure there was a bird trapped in our room somewhere."

Star giggled. "We all had to look in our desks and move all the book boxes and stuff and Billy kept tweet-tweeting in different places. He was adorable. Rolf reminds me of him a lot."

"I'm not sure if he can make animal noises," I said.

"Well, he's very talented in other ways," Star said.

Just then Francine came in and went to the mirror to reverse her earrings so they'd hang better.

"Wow, Janet!" she said. "Now I see why you like the little guy. He's a star!"

I almost said, "And now I see how you got a date, Francine Grady. He's your own cousin!" But I didn't. When you're feeling good, it's easier not to be mean.

"You're wrong, Francine," I said instead. It was actually unbelievable that I could sound so nonchalant when I had just discovered a startling truth. "I like Rolf because he's not the Paladin, or the Fantasy Lover, or even the Marlboro man. He's real. So what if he turned out to be a star? That's just . . . just . . ."

"Just the frosting on the cake?" Star asked.

Karen beamed. "On the *carrot* cake?"

We began to giggle, and Francine looked baffled. Then she shrugged. "Anyway, Janet. Getting HIM to take you to the dance was a real coup."

I smiled sweetly. "You know what, Francine? This time, you're right."

ABOUT THE AUTHOR

EVE BUNTING is the author of *Karen Kepplewhite Is the World's Best Kisser*, a companion volume to *Janet Hamm Needs a Date for the Dance*, as well as *Face at the Edge of the World* and *Someone Is Hiding on Alcatraz Island*. She lives in Pasadena, California.

BANTAM
SHOP-AT-HOME
C·A·T·A·L·O·G

Shop at home
for quality children's books
and save money, too.

Now you can order books for the whole family from Bantam's latest catalog of hundreds of titles including many fine children's books. *And* this special offer gives you an opportunity to purchase a Bantam book for only 50¢. Here's how:

By ordering any five books at the regular price per order, you can also choose any other single book listed (up to a $5.95 value) for just 50¢. Some restrictions do apply, so for further details send for Bantam's catalog of titles today.